AT THE EDGE

AT THE EDGE

A ROBYN HUNTER MYSTERY

NORAH McCLINTOCK

MINNEAPOLIS

First U.S. edition published in 2013 by Lerner Publishing Group, Inc.

Text copyright © 2009 by Norah McClintock. All rights reserved.
Published by arrangement with Scholastic Canada Ltd.

Darby Creek
A division of Lerner Publishing Group, Inc.
241 First Avenue North
Minneapolis, MN 55401 U.S.A.

Website address: www.lernerbooks.com

The images in this book are used with the permission of:
Front cover: © Peeter Viisimaa/Vetta/Getty Images;
© iStockphoto.com/Jaroslaw Wojcik, (boy).

Main body text set in Janson Text Lt Std 11.5/15.
Typeface provided by Linotype AG.

Library of Congress Cataloging-in-Publication Data

McClintock, Norah.
    At the edge / Norah McClintock. — 1st U.S. ed.
        p.   cm. — (Robyn Hunter mysteries ; #9)
    ISBN 978–0–7613–8319–2 (lib. bdg. : alk. paper)
    [1. Mystery and detective stories.] I. Title.
PZ7.M478414184So 2013
[Fic]—dc2   2012017533

Manufactured in the United States of America
1 – BP – 12/31/12

CHAPTER **ONE**

The way I had imagined it, the first few weeks in September would be pure heaven, total bliss, life as it should be—well, apart from having to go back to school.

The source of all this potential happiness? I would be staying with my father while the renovations to my mother's house, which had started during the summer, were finally completed. But, much as I love my dad, it wasn't the prospect of his company that filled me with joy. I was looking forward to a few weeks at my dad's place because that meant that I would be able to see Nick every day. Nick lives in an apartment on the second floor of my dad's building. My dad is his landlord.

But, as is so often the case where Nick is involved, things did not go according to plan. The morning of my first day with my father—also the first day of the school year—found me bending over in the park across the street from my dad's building, hand thrust deep into a plastic bag so that I could pick up after Nick's enormous black dog, Orion.

The city's poop-and-scoop law is one of the two reasons I have never wanted a dog. The other reason: a serious case of dog phobia brought on by a nasty bite when I was in elementary school. But I made an exception for Orion. I had agreed to take him out first thing in the morning so that Nick could get an hour or so of sleep before school.

Nick lives on his own. He supports himself. And since the middle of summer, he had been working to the point of exhaustion. He had a part-time job washing dishes at La Folie, the restaurant that occupies the ground floor of my father's building, and he took a second job as a night janitor at a mall. The way he had things mapped out for the foreseeable future: he would put in three or four shifts a week at the mall, usually from ten at night until six in the morning. If he had school the next day, he would dash home and grab a couple of hours of sleep before dragging himself out of bed and going to class.

Nick goes to an alternative school that caters to kids like him—who have been in trouble with the law, who come from messed-up families, who live by themselves or in group homes. It has a more flexible schedule than a regular school—it has to.

I couldn't imagine him keeping up the pace for long. I guess he couldn't either, because he kept saying it was just temporary. I felt bad that he had to work so hard, which is why I offered to help.

So there I was, trying not to gag as I picked up after Orion and wondered where Nick was. He hadn't been home when I'd gone downstairs to get the big dog. My question was answered when a sleek silver Lexus pulled up to the curb across the street and Nick got out. I raised my hand to wave to him, but I guess he didn't see me, because he headed straight for the door to my dad's building. Poor guy. He was probably exhausted. While he was digging his keys out of his pocket, the driver's-side door opened and a stunning blonde got out. She called to Nick. He turned and went back to the car, and she handed him something—I couldn't see what it was. Nick glanced at it and stuffed whatever it was into his jeans pocket. The girl said something else and then went up on tiptoe and kissed him on the cheek. My mouth gaped. Why was a beautiful blonde in a Lexus kissing my boyfriend? More importantly, why was he letting her?

The girl was smiling when she slid back in behind the wheel. She waved at Nick and drove away. Nick turned again to go inside. I couldn't decide what to do. Should I call to him and demand to know what was going on? Or should I—

Rowf!

That's all it took—the rumble of Orion's deep

doggy voice caught Nick's attention. He darted across the street and squatted beside me, scratching Orion behind the ears.

"So who was that?" I said in what I hoped was a casual tone.

Nick grinned as the big dog flipped over onto his back to get his belly scratched. "You mean Danny?"

"Danny?" I was confused. He said it as if I should know what he was talking about. *Wait a minute.* "Danny from work?"

"Yeah."

"Danny your friend, the one who got you the job at the mall?"

"Yeah. I told you about her."

That was true—sort of.

"You told me a friend named Danny worked at the mall and got you a job there," I said. "You never said Danny was a girl." Especially not a drop-dead gorgeous one. In fact, apart from a couple of brief mentions, he'd barely talked about Danny at all. Not that I'd asked—why would I?

"What difference does it make?" Nick said.

She'd kissed him. That's what difference it made.

"You said your friend Danny worked as a janitor with you."

"Yeah." He tried without success to stifle a yawn.

"You expect me to believe that girl is a janitor?" She looked more like a model. And what kind of mall janitor drove a Lexus?

"She was, but she isn't anymore," Nick said. "She was just there for the summer." Nick had spent the first part of the summer in a small town north of the city, near where I'd been working at a small local newspaper. He'd spent the rest of the summer back in the city, first recuperating from a gunshot wound and then working at the mall, driving a floor polisher. "Her dad owns the company that has the contract to clean the mall."

"So your friend Danny is the boss's daughter?"

"Yeah. But she's cool. She never acts like she's anything special. All summer she worked as hard as anyone else—maybe harder."

"How come she suddenly decided to drive you home?"

Nick gave me a look.

"She's been driving me home ever since I got the job," he said. That was news to me too. "Today was her last day. Her parents don't want her to work during the school year. They want her to concentrate on homework and stuff."

Judging by the car she drove, she probably didn't need to work during the summer either. Whatever. I was glad she was past tense. I didn't want to think about Nick spending every night with a coworker who looked like she belonged in a fashion layout.

"I saw her give you something," I said, still trying to sound casual.

"She got a new phone. She gave me the number."

I didn't like the sound of that, but I bit my tongue.

Nick took Orion's leash from me.

"I gotta go, Robyn. I gotta grab some sleep before school."

He loped back across the street.

"You're welcome," I muttered as I watched him go.

CHAPTER **TWO**

When I caught up with Morgan and Billy at school just before the bell rang, they were so tightly wrapped around each other that, from a distance, they looked like one person. The two of them had been inseparable ever since Billy got back from his summer job as a camp counselor. They had also been in almost nonstop physical contact with each other. They were my best friends—they had been for practically my whole life. But I was getting tired of watching them kissing and cuddling and beaming at each other like they were the only two people in the world who knew what love was, especially since I hardly ever saw Nick.

I took another look at Morgan and Billy and turned to walk away. Morgan chose that exact moment to come up for air.

"Hey, Robyn," she called to me. She still had one arm around Billy's waist and looked ridiculously happy.

"How was your weekend? You and Nick do anything special?"

"Not really," I said. "What about you guys? Did you have a good time?" Morgan and Billy had gone up to Morgan's summerhouse with her parents for the Labor Day weekend. They had invited me along, but I had stayed in town in hopes that I could get together with Nick. It hadn't worked out that way. Nick had pulled double shifts at La Folie and worked every night at the mall.

Morgan giggled. "We had a great time, didn't we, Billy?" she said.

Billy nodded. His grin was almost as wide as hers.

"But you saw Nick, right?" Morgan said.

"Not exactly."

"Not exactly?" Morgan's grin faded. "You either saw him or you didn't, Robyn."

"I didn't."

"You mean you spent the last weekend of the summer alone?" She looked shocked. "You should have come with us."

I was glad I hadn't. The only thing more depressing than not seeing Nick would have been not seeing Nick and spending the weekend watching Morgan and Billy snuggle.

The bell rang, and we went our separate ways. I didn't catch up with Morgan again until an hour later, after we had been to our homerooms and picked up our class schedules. Morgan was still beaming even though

Billy was nowhere to be seen.

"Guess what?" she said. She didn't give me a chance to answer. "Billy is in four of my classes this year. And his locker is right next to mine." She was ecstatic. "What about you? Let me see your schedule." I showed it to her and watched her face collapse. "Apart from social studies, you're not in any of my classes," she said. At least she still cared enough about me to be disappointed. "Where's your locker?"

"First floor, east wing. Yours?"

"Second floor, west wing," she said miserably.

"There's always lunch," I said.

We headed for the main doors. Morgan came to a sudden stop outside the school office.

"Who's that?" She pointed to a boy standing at the counter inside, talking to the vice principal. He was tall and sturdy-looking, with dark hair. "He must be new. For sure I would remember if I'd seen him before."

"He's in my homeroom," I said. Morgan's gaze shifted from the boy in the office to me.

"And?" Her eyes sparkled with interest. Morgan and Billy had been together for nearly a year, but that hadn't stopped Morgan from checking out every cute guy who stumbled into range.

"And what?"

"What do you mean, 'and what?' Look at him." She peered hungrily into the glass-fronted office. I grabbed her arm and started to drag her away before anyone noticed her blatant ogling.

"You're with Billy, remember?" I said.

She got that familiar faraway look in her eyes. "Billy is so sweet," she said with a sigh. But she cast another longing look over her shoulder as I pulled her down the hall.

"His name is James Derrick," I said. "He's a transfer student. That's all I know."

"And he's in your homeroom," Morgan said.

Like I cared.

. . .

Morgan was all aflutter as we walked together to the east wing of the school's main floor the next morning.

"Look whose locker is right across from yours," she said. "Oh my god, Robyn, he's totally adorable. You know, if things aren't working out with you and Nick—"

"I never said they weren't working out. I said things would be a lot easier if Nick wasn't working two jobs."

"No kidding," Morgan said. "Two jobs plus school doesn't leave much time for a girlfriend."

I shot her a sour look.

"You know what they say about a bird in the hand, Robyn." She beamed at James Derrick. He smiled shyly at her before closing his locker and heading down the hall.

"I wonder how he got that limp," she said.

I had wondered the same thing when he'd walked into homeroom the day before. It was slight but noticeable.

"Not that it matters," Morgan continued. "Not with a face like that. If I were you—"

"You're not me, Morgan," I said, my tone making it clear, I hoped, that the subject was closed.

.   .   .

I found Morgan and Billy in the cafeteria at lunch, and for once they weren't stuck to each other. I slipped into one of the two empty chairs opposite them.

"Guess what?" Morgan said. But something caught her eye before she could tell me. She jumped to her feet and waved. "James," she called. "Over here."

I glowered at her. "Morgan, I told you I wasn't inter—"

"Relax, Robyn," Morgan said. "James is in our French class. He doesn't know anyone yet. We invited him to have lunch with us."

"We?" I glanced at Billy.

"Morgan's idea," he said defensively. He could always tell when I was suspicious of Morgan's motives. Morgan glared at him. "But he seems nice," Billy added quickly. "He volunteered at an animal shelter before he moved here, and the first thing he did when he got to town was sign up to volunteer at the Humane Society."

That would pretty much make him perfect in Billy's eyes. Billy was a devoted animal rights activist.

Morgan watched James's every step as he navigated his way through the crowded cafeteria. He greeted

Morgan and Billy and then looked shyly at me.

"This is our friend Robyn Hunter," Morgan said.

"I know," James said. He had obviously been paying attention in homeroom. "Are you the Robyn Hunter who's at the top of the honor roll?"

Morgan tried to hide her irritation.

"Yes, she is," she said. Morgan usually topped the honor roll, but every now and then I edged her out. When I did, she always congratulated me. But Morgan is competitive, and I knew that she secretly wished her name had come first again last year. "I'm surprised you noticed something like that," she added.

"I didn't," James said. "But my dad did. The honor roll was the first thing he looked at when we came to register me for school."

I peeled the lid off a yogurt container and kept my head down while I ate. Billy quizzed James about what he was doing at the animal shelter and filled him in on DARC, a bird-rescue organization that Billy had founded. While they talked, Morgan leaned across the table and whispered in my ear: "He'd be perfect for you. He'd be perfect for us. We'd make an amazing foursome . . ."

I shook my head impatiently and felt glad when lunch was over.

CHAPTER **THREE**

"You should come," Morgan said when she phoned me the next night.

"I don't know." I was lying on the bed in the room my dad had set aside for me, my phone pressed to my ear.

"Come on, it'll be fun, Robyn."

"It'll be depressing."

The "it" in question was a screening of a new documentary about climate change that was being held at our school on Friday night. Billy had helped to organize it. Normally I wouldn't have hesitated to say yes, even if the topic was a total downer. But despite knowing Morgan and Billy practically forever, lately when I was with them, I felt like a third wheel.

"Why don't you ask James to come?" Morgan said.

That again. She kept mentioning James.

"Because I'm going out with Nick," I said as patiently as I could manage.

"Are you going out with him on Friday night?"

I had been hoping to. Nick hadn't been scheduled to work at the mall on Friday. But then he'd accepted an extra shift at La Folie. "I need the money, Robyn," he'd said.

"He has to work," I told Morgan.

"All the more reason to ask James."

"No."

"Okay, okay. But at least come to the movie. Please?"

"I don't know, Morgan—"

"Come on, Robyn. Nick works practically every night. Are you going to give up on a social life just because he isn't around? Come to the movie. We'll do something afterward."

. . .

Morgan was waiting for me on the school steps on Friday evening, and we went into the auditorium together. A lot of people had turned out for the movie. But I noticed that more than half the audience was made up of adults. When I mentioned it to Morgan, she just shrugged.

"Billy doesn't care who sees the movie as long as people show up."

I glanced up at the front of the auditorium, where Billy was talking to Mr. Henson, the biology teacher who had arranged for Billy to use the auditorium and helped to publicize the event. Billy scanned the room happily as people continued to trickle in.

Morgan and I had just found seats when, without warning, she rammed an elbow into my side.

"Hey!" I said.

"Look who's coming up the aisle," Morgan whispered.

I turned, hoping against hope that it was Nick.

It was James. I looked suspiciously at Morgan.

"Did you invite him?" I asked.

"No. I swear."

Her face was the picture of innocence. Either she was telling the truth or she had evolved into a champion liar. She stood up and called to him. "Hey, James, over here!"

James turned in our direction, but it took a moment for him to locate us. He smiled shyly when he spotted Morgan and started making his way toward us. Morgan moved over one seat so that he could sit between us.

"It's a surprise to see you here," she said, mostly, I think, to prove she hadn't known he was coming.

"Well, I care about the environment," he said. "And my dad's been on my case ever since we moved in. He says the only way I'm going to meet people and make friends is if I get out and make an effort."

"It must be hard, moving to a new city and having to meet all new people," Morgan said.

"It's not exactly new," James said. "I grew up here— well, in the west end. We moved away a few years ago, and now we're back. But I lost touch with most of the kids I used to know, so . . ."

The auditorium lights blinked on and off a few times, a sign that the movie was about to start. Billy stood up on the stage and reached for a microphone. He thanked everyone for coming, talked a little about the movie we were going to see, and said that there would be collection buckets at the doors afterwards so that anyone who was interested could make a donation to an organization that did climate-change work. Then the lights went down and the movie started.

When it was over, Morgan said, "We're going out for something to eat, James. Do you want to come along?"

I glared at her to let her know how I felt about this little surprise. She didn't flinch.

"How about it?" she said, smiling unwaveringly at James.

"Well, I—" He looked awkwardly at me.

"You want to get to know people better, right?" Morgan said. "So come on. Get to know us."

"Okay," James said. "I just have to make a quick phone call." He stepped away from us so that he could have some privacy. While we waited, Morgan and I helped Billy collect donations. Billy was delighted when he found out that Morgan had invited James to come out with us. The two of them seemed to have plenty in common.

We walked a couple of blocks to a vegan restaurant that Billy adored and that made excellent soy shakes. Afterwards, James offered me a ride home.

"It's kind of out of the way," I said. My dad lived farther from the school than my mother did.

"All the more reason for me to give you a lift," he said.

"That's really nice of James, isn't it, Robyn?" Morgan said, jabbing me with her elbow again. One more time and she was going to leave a bruise.

I scowled at her.

"If you'd rather not . . ." James said. Great. I was making him feel bad, and he wasn't the person I was annoyed with.

"A ride would be nice, thanks," I said. Morgan beamed at me. I gave her a warning look. But that didn't stop her from giving me a double thumbs-up when I turned to walk with James to his car. I was going to have to have another talk with her. Nick's name would feature prominently.

James's car had seen better days.

"It's not much to look at," he said apologetically. "But it gets me where I need to go."

He followed my directions to my dad's building.

"Sorry, what?" I said after we had been on the road for a few uncomfortable minutes. James had mostly been silent, but once, when I glanced at him, I'd seen his lips moving, and then I had heard him mutter something. Had he been talking to me?

James glanced at me, a startled look on his face.

"Did you just say something about bread?" I said.

His cheeks flushed with embarrassment.

"Bread, milk, and, most important, the decaf?" he said. "Sorry. I just don't want to forget."

"Forget what?"

"What I'm supposed to pick up on the way home. For my dad."

He brought the car to a stop in front of La Folie. My heart raced when I saw Nick standing out on the sidewalk. He was wearing a white apron over black jeans and a white T-shirt. *He must be on a break*, I thought. I was just about to get out of the car and go over to him when a man and a girl came out of the restaurant. I recognized the girl immediately. Danny. Nick broke into a smile when he saw her. The man smiled, too, and shook Nick's hand. They chatted for a few moments. Nick seemed relaxed with the man—he must have known the guy for a while. Because of his past, Nick was naturally cautious and mistrustful. It took him a while to warm up to new people.

"Robyn?" James touched my arm.

"Huh?" I'd forgotten for a moment that I wasn't alone.

"I was just saying that I had a good time. Morgan and Billy are a lot of fun." He frowned slightly. "Is everything okay?"

"Fine," I said. "I was just thinking about something. I'm sorry. I had a good time, too." I glanced out the window again. Danny and the man were walking down the street. I waited until they got into the same silver Lexus I had seen on the first day of school before I said, "Thanks for the lift." I got out of James's car just as the Lexus roared away down the street.

Nick looked surprised to see me step out onto the sidewalk. He checked out James's car and ducked down a little so that he could see who was driving.

"Who was that?" he said after James had pulled away from the curb.

"Just a guy from my school."

"Yeah?" He glanced at the car's disappearing tail-lights. "What were you two up to?"

"I told you," I said. "Billy was screening a movie at school tonight. I invited you to come."

Nick's eyes hardened. "And when I couldn't make it, you invited another guy?"

"No. James just showed up."

"And then he drove you home?"

"Yes, he did. But that shouldn't be a big deal for you, right? I mean, Danny drove you home all summer."

Anger flared in Nick's eyes. I could see he was making an effort to hide what he was feeling.

"Well, at least he's not one of those rich kids," he said. I had gone out briefly with a guy named Ben Logan whose dad was extremely wealthy. Nick had commented more than once on what it must have been like to be with someone who could afford to take me anywhere and buy me anything. Sometimes I thought he didn't believe me when I told him I didn't care about money.

"Didn't I just see Danny leave—in her Lexus?"

Nick bristled. "It's her dad's car."

"Is that the man who was with her?"

Nick nodded.

"So Danny and her dad just happened to come to La Folie tonight, when you just happened to be working a last-minute shift?"

"I've been telling Danny about the place. Her mom was at some charity thing tonight, so she and her dad came for dinner. He's a really nice guy."

"It looked like the three of you had a terrific time." And yes, I know how I probably sounded—angry and jealous.

Nick's expression softened a little.

"I didn't have dinner with them, Robyn. I've been in the kitchen all night, working. I just talked to them for a minute on their way out."

"When do you get off?" I said, suddenly feeling childish at the way I had reacted.

"Not 'til after closing."

I groaned. La Folie's kitchen closed at midnight, and then Nick had to do cleanup.

"I'll call you tomorrow, okay?" he said.

"Okay." And it really seemed okay, especially when he kissed me lightly on the cheek before darting down the alley and letting himself in through the kitchen door.

CHAPTER **FOUR**

Nick called, as he had promised, but not until midafternoon.

"You want to come up here?" I said.

"I just woke up," he said, "and I have a ton of homework to do before I have to be at the mall."

"Okay. I'll come down and keep you company."

There was a moment's hesitation before he said, "I really have to concentrate."

"I'll be quiet, I promise. I'll bring my homework. We can work together."

"Okay," Nick said. He didn't sound nearly as enthusiastic as I would have liked.

I gathered up my things and went down to his apartment. Nick was dressed but barefoot, and his hair was sticking out in every direction like he'd been struck by lightning. Textbooks were spread all over his small kitchen table. He sat down and bent over them. I made some room for myself.

"Are you hungry?" I said after a couple of minutes. "Want me to make you something to eat?"

He looked up from the textbook he was reading.

"No, it's okay," he said. "I had some cereal."

He started to read again. His face was so serious.

"How about some tea or hot chocolate?" I said.

"No, I'm okay, thanks." He didn't even look up this time.

I opened my history book. I had a whole chapter to read and make notes on. But I couldn't take my eyes off Nick. I had barely spent any time with him since I'd come back from up north. I missed him.

"Let's take a break," I said. "We can take Orion for a walk."

Nick's eyes flashed with annoyance. "I told you, Robyn. I have to get this done. But I can't concentrate when you keep interrupting me."

"Sorry." I forced myself to read a few paragraphs. Then: "It's just that I never see you anymore."

Nick's head bobbed up again. "Maybe it's better if I study alone. I'll get it done faster."

"I'm sorry," I said again. "I promise I'll be quiet."

Nick stood up, exasperated. "You want to do something helpful? How about if you take Orion for a walk? Otherwise he'll be cooped up in here all day." Without waiting for an answer, he retrieved the big dog's leash from a hook next to the apartment door. As soon as Orion heard the jingle of the chain, he started to bark excitedly.

"Come with me," I said to Nick.

"I can't." He snapped the leash to the dog's collar. "You be good for Robyn," he told the dog. "No chasing squirrels."

Over by the couch, his phone rang.

"Now what?" Nick said. He handed me the leash and dashed into the living room to answer the phone. He growled a gruff hello, and I felt sorry for whoever was on the other end of the line—until his expression softened and he said, "Danny, hi. No, not much. Just trying to get my homework done."

Danny again.

She must have said something funny, because Nick laughed.

"No, I'm not kidding," he said. "I'm really doing homework." He glanced up and seemed surprised to find me still standing there. He covered the phone's receiver. "I'll see you when you get back," he said. "And make it a nice long walk, okay, Robyn? I haven't been able to take him out as much as I'd like to."

I was fuming as I made my way downstairs with the dog. Nick had been impatient with my interruption but not with Danny's. He was happy enough to have me walk his dog and pick up after him, but he never seemed to be able to find time to spend with me. It wasn't fair. And he didn't even apologize when I brought Orion back an hour later.

"Homework done?" I said.

He nodded.

"So now do you want to do something?"

"I'm working today."

"You don't start for hours."

"I have to go by Danny's place first."

"Danny's place? Since when?"

"Since she called me. Her dad is having some people over for a barbecue this afternoon. He invited me. Don't give me that look, Robyn. This could be good for me. He wants to introduce me to someone."

"Who?"

"He has a friend who's a vet."

"A veterinarian?"

Nick nodded.

"Is something wrong with Orion? Is he sick?"

"No, but . . ." He shrugged awkwardly.

"But what?"

"I mentioned to Danny over the summer how I was kind of thinking how cool it would be to be a vet—"

"Since when have you been thinking that?" I said. It was the first I had heard of it.

"For a while." He sounded defensive. "I didn't say anything to you about it because my grades haven't been that great. You need math and science and stuff like that. I thought you'd laugh at me."

"I've never laughed at you, Nick." It was true. I never had. But that didn't stop him from feeling self-conscious sometimes.

"Anyway," he said, "Mr. Vitali said he wanted to introduce me to this vet friend of his. He said he would be able to give me a good idea of what's involved."

"What about work?"

"Danny's going to drive me after."

Danny—always Danny. I didn't know her. I hadn't even met her. But already I didn't like her.

Nick took Orion's leash from me and handed me my schoolbooks.

"I have to get changed," he said. "Danny's picking me up in ten minutes."

"Will I see you tomorrow?" I said.

"I'm scheduled to work downstairs. But I'll call you if I get a chance."

If?

I dumped my books upstairs and called Morgan. She was at Billy's house. They were doing homework together.

"You want to come over?" she said.

I thought about her and Billy snuggling with each other and me all alone.

"No, it's okay," I said. "I'll talk to you tomorrow."

I sat in the window in my father's living room and looked down at the street. It wasn't long before a silver Lexus pulled up. Nick darted toward it. His hair was neatly combed. He climbed into the front seat, and the car drove off.

I spent Saturday night alone.

Nick called me the next night, but when I saw on my phone's display that it was him, I didn't answer. I was still mad that he'd had time for Danny but not for me.

. . .

On Monday morning, my dad was up before me, as usual.

"Breakfast?" he said with a cheeriness that I found irritating.

"I have to walk Orion," I said.

"No, you don't. Nick was up here half an hour ago. He said to tell you he had it under control."

"Why didn't you call me?"

"You were asleep."

"Why didn't you wake me?"

"Nick asked me not to."

"He didn't want to talk to me?"

"He didn't want to disturb you." Dad looked closely at me. "Is everything okay between you two?"

"I don't know. I hardly ever see him."

My dad gave me a sympathetic look. "I know how that goes," he said. The number-one reason my parents had divorced was that my dad, who used to be a cop, was rarely home. It used to drive my mom crazy, especially when she went back to school to get her law degree. She had expected Dad to be home more often so that she could study, but it hadn't turned out that way. "Nick has a lot on his plate, Robbie. He has to worry about things you never even have to think about."

I knew that, but it didn't help, especially now that Danny was on the scene.

CHAPTER **FIVE**

I spotted James before he even noticed I was there. He was at his locker, engrossed in whatever he was holding in his hand. As I got closer, I saw that it was a phone. But he wasn't making a call.

"Get a new app or something?" I said.

He jumped, startled, and then slid his phone shut and jammed it into his pocket before I could see what he'd been doing.

"I was just checking something," he said. He busied himself at his own locker, but he kept glancing furtively at me while I unpacked my backpack and sorted out what I needed for my first couple classes.

"Is something wrong?" I said finally.

His face flushed. "What do you mean?"

"You're staring at me."

His cheeks turned even redder. "I'm sorry," he said. He looked down at the floor.

Whatever. I got my things out of my locker. I was locking up again when he said, "I have to ask you something."

Please, please, please, do not ask me out, I thought. I turned and waited.

"I should have kept my mouth shut, but I didn't. I'm sorry, Robyn."

Sorry? What was he talking about? There were another few agonizing moments of silence.

"I told my dad about you," he said at last. "I—I mentioned that you were in my homeroom and that we have a class together."

"Okay," I said slowly. I wished he would get to the point.

"The thing is, he remembered you."

"Remembered me?" I said. "I've never met your dad, James."

"I know." He sounded miserable. "But he remembered your name from the honor roll outside the school office."

I nodded. "And?"

"And he told me to ask you. If I don't, he'll just bug me about it, and then he'll probably call you and ask you himself. He can be really persistent."

I was obviously going to have to nudge him to find out what he was talking about.

"Ask me what, James?"

"You don't have to say yes. I can tell him that you're too busy."

"Too busy for what?"

He finally met my eyes.

"I was in an accident. I missed a lot of school because of it. I should have graduated a year ago. And . . . I don't know, my grades used to be okay, but lately . . ." Poor James. He was one of those people who turn splotchy when they get embarrassed. It was agonizing to watch his face flush redder and redder as he struggled with what he was trying to say. "My dad has a PhD. Education is important to him. He always told me and G—" He broke off and shook his head, as if he were mad at himself for something. "He always made it clear that he expected me to continue my education after high school. But the way things have been going . . ."

I glanced surreptitiously at my watch. The homeroom bell was going to ring any moment.

"What is it you want to ask me, James?"

"It was a mistake to mention that I'd met you. As soon as I did, he started bugging me. He's like that. He always tries to find out who's the best and then he goes after that person."

"Best person for what?"

"My dad thinks I need a tutor. He said he was going to call the school to see if they would recommend someone. Then, when I mentioned you, he said you would be perfect." He hung his head again. "I really want to catch up. I want to graduate and go to college—just maybe not for the reasons my father wants me to go." When he looked at me there was a fierce expression on his face. "I need to get away. And, for that I need good grades."

The determined look on his face convinced me that he meant what he was saying. It also told me there was some kind of friction between James and his father. Maybe it was as simple as a high-achieving parent expecting too much from his son. Or maybe it was something else. Either way, I felt sorry for James. He was so quiet and shy, and he seemed nice enough. Still . . .

"I don't know, James. To be honest, I've never tutored anyone before."

"Forget I mentioned it," he said, his cheeks blazing.

"I mean, I'd probably be no good at it."

"It's okay. It was my dad's idea, not mine."

"I know there are kids here who tutor. I bet if your dad calls the guidance counselor's office, they can put him in touch with someone."

"Sure. I'll tell him."

"I'm sorry, James, but—"

"It's no big deal," he said. "Forget it."

. . .

I had free period at the end of the day. Instead of going to the library or heading home, I jumped onto the bus and rode across town to the small alternative school that Nick attends. It's located above a strip of stores on a busy downtown street. I got there just as the students were leaving for the day. At first I was afraid I had missed Nick, but then there he was, coming through the door with a bunch of his friends. I smiled tentatively at him—was he still mad at me? He smiled back, and relief flooded through me. Then I saw a familiar face.

Danny.

I froze.

Nick strode across the sidewalk to me.

"Hey, what are you doing here?" he said. He was still smiling, which I took as a good sign. "I called you yesterday, but you didn't answer."

I glanced at Danny. She had paused along with the rest of Nick's group. They were all watching us.

"Come on," Nick said, taking me by the hand. "We're going out to get something to eat. I'll introduce you to everyone."

He didn't give me a chance to say no, not that I would have. He led me back to his friends and introduced me around—as his friend Robyn, not his girlfriend.

We walked to a restaurant a few doors down from the school. I'm not even sure how it happened, but Danny ended up sitting beside Nick, and I ended up across from her. Another girl—the only other girl in the bunch—was wedged in next to me. Nick introduced her as Jenn, but she didn't even look at me, let alone talk to me.

"Where do you go to school, Robyn?" Danny said. She had sparkling pale blue eyes, a heart-shaped face with a clear complexion, and a mass of blonde hair that fell in waves over her shoulders. She was even prettier up close than she had appeared from across the street.

When I answered her question, a couple of the kids

at the table glanced at Nick as if they were wondering how he had hooked up with someone like me. What was the matter? Was my school poison?

"I have a cousin who got expelled from there," someone said.

"Oh." I didn't know what else to say.

"The principal's a real tool," the same person said. "My cousin says the whole place is full of tools."

Right. His cousin, who had been expelled, was an excellent judge of the student body at my school. I glanced at Nick. He mumbled something about my dad being his landlord. What was going on? He actually looked embarrassed. After a few moments of silence, a server showed up to take our orders. Then everyone started talking about teachers I didn't know, people I had never heard of, and stuff they had been involved in. Most of the kids at Nick's school were like Nick; most had been in some kind of trouble. A lot of them had been kicked out of their original schools. I looked across the table at Nick, but he was laughing at something Danny had said. Finally, mercifully, everyone finished eating and went their separate ways.

"Can I give you a ride home, Nick?" Danny said.

"You can give us both a ride," Nick said. "We'd really appreciate it, right, Robyn?"

I would have preferred that Danny just get lost, but of course that didn't happen.

Nick rode up front. I was stuck in the backseat. Nick and Danny chatted the whole way. At first I was surprised by how much she seemed to know about him. Then I found out that she was more than the boss's daughter—much more.

"Remember that time you and Joey decided to build a tree house in the courtyard?" Danny said. "You guys scrounged wood and tools from everyone in the building. Even Mr. Siroka gave you some good stuff."

"Who's Mr. Siroka?" I said.

"The super at our building," Danny said.

Our building?

"You gotta admit, it was a good-looking tree house," Nick said.

"It sure was. And remember how you two had that big argument about who got to go in it first?"

Nick laughed. "I still can't figure out if Joey let me go first because he was being nice or because he suspected what was going to happen."

"It's a good thing you guys didn't build it any higher," Danny said, laughing again. "Somebody could have got hurt."

"It's a good thing I didn't get all the way inside before it tipped over."

"It's also a good thing that I was the only person out in the courtyard that morning."

"And that you weren't standing too close," Nick said.

Danny laughed. "I still remember the look on your face as you dangled from that branch, looking down at the smashed tree house on the ground below you."

"All that work," Nick said.

"I wish I'd taken a picture," Danny said.

I had never heard Nick laugh so hard. It took a few moments for him to stop.

"I'm really glad we ran into each other again, Nick," Danny said, glancing at him. Had she forgotten that I was sitting right behind her?

"Me, too," Nick said. He had a warm, soft expression on his face as he looked at her. I was glad when she finally pulled up in front of my dad's building.

"See you at school," she said as Nick climbed out of the car and pushed the front seat forward so that I could get out. Danny ducked down a little so that she could see his face. "I never thought I would be saying that to you again," she said.

Nick smiled and waved to her as she drove away.

"You didn't tell me that Danny goes to your school," I said as her car disappeared around the corner. I tried to sound casual, as if it were no big deal.

"She doesn't."

"But she just said—"

"She goes to one of those private schools where the kids' parents are all loaded."

"I thought you didn't like private-school kids." He had certainly given me a hard time about Ben, who went to the most exclusive boys' school in the city.

"I don't," Nick said. "But Danny is different. She didn't start out rich. She's a real person. And her school does some good things. They have this program where kids volunteer at schools in disadvantaged neighborhoods."

"Volunteer to do what?"

"They show up a couple of times a week and help with homework or assignments or whatever."

"She volunteers at your school?"

"Yeah."

"A couple of times a week?"

"Yeah."

"Well, that'll be nice for you."

"Yeah, it will," Nick said. "Danny is really smart. And we've known each other since forever."

"So I gather," I said. "You didn't mention that either."

"I told you she was a friend."

"You didn't say she was such an old friend."

"Yeah, well, she is. She used to live in my building. I was really sorry when she moved out."

"I bet."

Nick gave me a sharp look. "I'm glad I ran into her again."

"So I noticed."

"What's the matter with you? You sound like you're jealous or something."

I was jealous. Danny was gorgeous. She knew things about Nick that I didn't know. She had gotten him a job. Her dad had obviously taken an interest in him. And now she was going to be at his school a couple of times a week. I was insanely jealous. But I wasn't going to tell Nick that.

"I am not jealous," I said.

"Well, good. Because Danny's an old friend. I like

her, Robyn. We were really close. So I don't want to have to feel guilty every time I see her."

It was so hard to picture Nick being close to anyone. I had known him for a little over a year—and he hadn't exactly opened up his life to me. I'd had to work hard to get him to trust me. I'd put up with a lot, too. And now here he was, laughing and chatting with another girl—one who had a completely different picture of him than I did. A girl who obviously made him feel safe and comfortable.

"If you need any help with homework or assignments, I could tutor you," I said.

"I don't need a tutor."

"But you just said that Danny and the kids from her school are at your school to help you."

"I said they were there to help anyone who needs help. I didn't say she was helping me. God, Robyn, for someone who isn't jealous, you're sure acting jealous." He glanced at his watch. "I gotta go. I want to walk Orion before work."

"I'll come with you."

"No, it's okay."

"But—"

"I need some down time, Robyn, some quiet time so I can think." He kissed me lightly on the cheek. "Okay?"

"Okay," I said, even though that wasn't what I meant. What did he have to think about? And why couldn't he think with me around?

· · ·

"Maybe Nick is telling the truth," Morgan said when I called to tell her what had happened. "Maybe they're just friends."

Maybe? I didn't like the sound of that. I was sitting in the window in my dad's living room, watching for Nick to come back from his walk with Orion.

"Well," Morgan said, hesitating—which was not a good sign. Morgan never hesitates unless she's trying to spare someone's feelings, which she rarely does.

"Well, what?" I prodded.

"He said he ran into her by accident, right?"

"You were there when he told me," I said testily. He'd mentioned it one weekend when he came up to Morgan's summerhouse.

"He never said Danny was a girl. In fact, as I recall, he didn't say much about her at all. He mostly talked about the job."

"So?" I said, even though I had been thinking the same thing.

"So, he runs into Danny, she arranges for Daddy to give him a job—at the same place where she's working. Then, as soon as summer's over, she volunteers for a program that means she'll be at his school a couple of times a week. And she invites him over for a barbecue. You can't help thinking—even if he sees her as just a friend, she seems to be making more than a friendly effort to be part of his life."

"I hope you're not trying to cheer me up, Morgan."

"You asked me what I thought, and I'm telling you. I'm being honest, Robyn."

One thing I've noticed: when people tell you they're being honest, it almost always hurts.

"What do you think I should do?" I said.

Morgan hesitated again.

"Well," she said, "he didn't tell you anything about her until you saw the two of them together. When you offered to help him with his homework, he turned you down. And you never see him anymore—you said so yourself, Robyn. Maybe he's trying to tell you something."

"Great. Thanks!"

"I'm just being—"

"Honest, I know. Honesty isn't always the best policy, Morgan."

"Would you rather I lied to you? What kind of friend would I be if I did that? Look, Robyn, if you want my opinion"—I wasn't sure I did—"maybe you should just back off for a while. Give Nick some space. Let him figure out what he wants."

"If Billy was spending more time with a gorgeous blonde than he was with you, is that what you'd do?"

"The great thing about Billy is that most of the people he hangs out with are total nerds," she said. "I really don't have to worry about other girls."

"What if you did have to worry? What if there was another girl?"

"I'd probably scratch her eyes out. At least, that's what I'd want to do." I didn't doubt that for a moment. "Why don't you show Nick how you feel?"

"What do you mean?"

"You don't like that he's spending so much of his spare time with this Danny person, right? How would he like it if you were spending time with another guy?"

"But I'm not."

"You could, though. James asked you to tutor him, right?"

"You know about that?"

"He mentioned it to Billy. He wanted to know what you'd say if he asked you."

"What did Billy tell him?"

"That you'd probably say yes. You did say yes, didn't you?"

"No."

"No, you didn't say yes?"

"Yes, I mean I said no."

"Well, say yes! Tell James you'll tutor him, and then let Nick know you're doing it."

"What good will that do?"

"For one thing, it will tell you if Nick still cares about you."

"If?" I was beginning to hate that word.

"That's what you're worried about, isn't it? If he gets mad or tells you that he doesn't want you to tutor James, you'll know that he still cares. Then you can relax."

"And if he doesn't get mad? If he doesn't care?"

"James seems really nice, Robyn. Billy likes him a lot. If you tutor him, you'll get to know him better. If things don't work out with Nick, you'll have a fallback position. It's a lot easier to get over a breakup if you're seeing someone else—especially someone as cute as James."

"I don't know," I said. Part of me agreed with Morgan—maybe I should give Nick a taste of his own medicine and see how he likes it. But mostly I was afraid that Nick wouldn't care.

"Well, do you have a better idea?" Morgan said.

I sat in the window for a long time after I had spoken to Morgan. Nick must have taken Orion in the back way, because the next time I saw him he was coming out the front door. If I hurried, maybe I could catch up to him. I jumped up—too late. Nick broke into a run as a bus rounded the corner. He made it to the bus door just in time and disappeared from sight.

CHAPTER SIX

James was already at his locker when I got to school the next morning. I marched up to him and said, "Okay, I'll do it."

He stared blankly at me.

"You want a tutor," I said. "You've got one."

"You mean it?" He sounded surprised. And pleased.

"We can start this afternoon if you want."

James smiled cautiously at me. "I really appreciate this," he said. "When I told my dad it didn't look like you were going to do it, he wanted to call you and ask you himself."

"Really?" I was a little taken aback. "I'm sure he would have had no problem finding someone else."

"You don't know my dad. I wasn't kidding about him. When he saw your name at the top of the honor roll, he decided you were the best. And my dad always goes after the best."

"You're making me nervous," I said. "I seriously have never tutored anyone before, James. I might turn out to be terrible."

He laughed. "The only way you could turn out to be terrible is if you know less about math and science than I do—and that doesn't seem likely. I'm glad you said yes, Robyn. I just hope you don't quit when you find out how dumb I am."

"There's a big difference between not knowing something and being dumb," I said. "I just hope I don't disappoint you."

He beamed at me. "There's no way you could do that."

Out of the corner of my eye, I saw Morgan. She had come down the hall and was standing a few lockers away, behind James. She was grinning like a lottery winner. I was surprised she wasn't also doing a happy dance.

.   .   .

James and I met after school, as we had arranged, and headed to the public library, where we sat together while he worked on his math homework. I could see why his dad was so eager to find him a tutor. James and I were in different math classes, but we had the same teacher, so I knew exactly what work he was supposed to do. I also knew that the work had been explained in detail during class. Even so, James struggled with his assignment. But he listened attentively to what I said and watched carefully while I worked on some examples for him. By the end of the hour he was making his way through the last of the exercises he had been assigned.

"You must think I'm a real moron," he said as he packed up his things.

"No, I don't," I said. "You did fine."

"Tell that to my dad." He slid the textbook and his binder into his backpack and zipped the pocket. "He says I'm the most absentminded person he knows. When I was younger and he'd send me on an errand, he used to make me repeat five times what I was supposed to do so that I wouldn't forget. He still makes me repeat stuff. He says it's the best way to remember."

"Bread, milk, and, most important, the decaf," I said.

His cheeks turned red.

I grinned at him. "You can tell your dad you did great. You probably just have to catch up. You said you missed a lot of school."

"I had a bad couple years after I left here, that's for sure," he said.

A couple of years?

"First my mother died."

"I'm sorry," I said.

"Then I was in an accident. I was in the hospital for months and then in rehab."

"God, James, that must have been awful."

He shrugged. "My dad says my main problem is that I don't focus. But that hasn't been my problem lately. Before my mom and the accident, I didn't care about school. I didn't care about anything."

He seemed like such a gentle, quiet guy. It was hard to imagine him not caring.

"But I care now," he added quickly. "I don't want you to think you're going to be wasting your time. I'm already a year behind. I want to get through this. I want to make the grades so that I have some options."

"If you keep working like you did today, you'll be fine," I said.

He smiled, and this time I saw how right Morgan was. He was extremely cute—and, unlike Nick, he was turning out to be open and easy to get to know. When he offered me a ride home, I accepted.

. . .

On my way up to my dad's place, I stopped and knocked on Nick's door. No answer. I could barely concentrate on my homework. Then my phone rang.

. . .

"So?" Morgan said the next morning. She was waiting for me outside school. "How did it go?"

"How did what go?"

"The tutoring. How was it? Did you have fun?"

"It was math, Morgan." I had actually enjoyed myself, which surprised me. But there was no way I was going to tell her that. She might get the wrong idea.

"But you're going to see him again, right?"

"I'm just tutoring him, Morgan. That's all. Besides," I added triumphantly, "Nick called last night. He invited me to a party." The downside: most of the people there would be kids from his school. The glorious upside: it would be the first carefree night I had spent with Nick since the summer. I could hardly wait.

Morgan didn't say a word. She didn't seem to be paying any attention, and she wasn't even looking at me. I turned to see what had caught her interest.

James. He was leaning against his car in the school parking lot.

"He's been staring at his phone for, like, five minutes now," Morgan said. "He does that a lot."

I had seen him staring at it once. But a lot?

"He's probably playing a game."

"I don't think so," Morgan said. "If he was playing a game, his thumbs would be moving. But he's just staring. I saw him doing it yesterday, too. Standing in the hall, staring at his phone. He didn't even notice when I went up to him. I'm not one hundred percent positive, but I think he was looking at pictures."

"Maybe they're pictures of friends back home. Or maybe his mom." I filled Morgan in on what little I knew.

"Well, whatever he's doing, he looks really down," she said.

Pictures of his mother, I decided.

"Let's cheer him up," Morgan said. She called his name and waved to him. His head bobbed up. He stuffed his phone into his pocket and made his way over to us.

His limp seemed more pronounced than usual.

"Hey, Robyn," he said, smiling shyly.

"What are you up to, James?" Morgan said.

The question seemed to startle him. His face turned red.

"Up to?" he said. "What do you mean?"

"She means, what's new?" I said, even though I knew that wasn't what she had meant at all. I shot her a look. She just shrugged. We all went into school together. But I couldn't help wondering what James had been looking at—and why he had been so startled by Morgan's question.

. . .

"Robbie, I was just going to call you," my dad said when I walked through the door after school. "Be an angel and let me borrow your car."

I stared at him. My dad always takes pride in his appearance. When he dresses up, he really dresses up. He has a closet full of expensive suits. When he dresses down, he still looks great. His jeans fit well. His T-shirts are strictly designer. His boots and shoes are well looked after. I had never seen my dad sloppy or unkempt—until today. He was wearing faded, grubby jeans; a shapeless T-shirt that appeared to have been dredged out of a thrift-store bin; battered work boots that looked as if a few different pairs of feet had tromped around in them; and a faded work shirt.

"Why are you dressed like that, Dad? And what happened to the Porsche?"

"The Porsche is fine, Robbie. I have a job, and if I don't punch in on time, I'm going to get into trouble on my first day."

"Punch in?" My dad has his own business. He's in private security and investigations. He has clients—plenty of them. But I had never heard of any of them putting him on a time clock. "What kind of job? Where?"

"Warehouse."

"You're working in a warehouse?"

"A lot of merchandise has gone missing," my father said. "They think it's an inside job."

"You're working undercover?"

My dad nodded. "I thought I could use your car. It fits the profile a lot better than mine does."

I had a beat-up Toyota that my future stepfather Ted had bought me for my summer job. I had barely driven it since returning to the city. I dug in my backpack for my keychain, removed my car keys, and tossed them to him.

"I'm going to be working nights for a couple of weeks at least," my dad said. "Maybe longer. It might be a good idea for you to move in with your mom and Ted until the house is ready. Otherwise you're going to be alone a lot."

I thought about being in close proximity to my mom while she was (a) working, (b) overseeing renovations that were already running late, and (c) planning her wedding, which was scheduled to take place in three months. I love my mother. I really do. But she's a Type-A personality at the best of times, and it was so peaceful at my dad's place.

"I'd rather stay here, Dad."

He looked doubtful. "We'll talk about it tomorrow, Robbie. I have to get going." He kissed me on the cheek and dashed out the door.

. . .

I met James the next day after school to help him with his homework. Morgan tagged along. The plan was that she would come to my dad's place with me afterwards and spend the night. When we got to the library, James and I settled at a large study table and Morgan found a spot at another table where we wouldn't disturb her, or vice versa. But the whole time she kept glancing at me and grinning.

This time things didn't go as well. James seemed distracted while I was explaining the work to him, and he had trouble applying what I'd shown him to the exercises he had been assigned.

"Is something wrong, James?" I said, trying to hide the exasperation I was feeling.

"What?" He blinked at me.

"Something about my explanation you don't understand?" So far he hadn't gotten a single right answer.

He looked sheepishly at me. "I'm sorry. I didn't get much sleep last night. I'll do better next time, I promise."

When he pushed back his chair to stand up, he knocked over his backpack. He ducked down, grabbed one of the straps, and hauled the pack up onto the table so that he could stuff his books into it. "Sorry," he said again.

"We can review the material one more time if you want," I said.

He shook his head. "I have an errand to do. I'll see you at school tomorrow."

I frowned as I watched him make his way to the elevator. What was bothering him?

I glanced at Morgan. She was staring at the elevators. It was a few moments before she got up and came over to where I was sitting. As I gathered my things, she dove down under the table.

"What are you doing?" I said.

Her head popped up. She glanced around.

"What's going on, Morgan?"

She straightened up, laid her hand on the table, and opened it. She was holding a phone.

"That isn't yours," I said. Morgan's phone was pink. The one in her hand was black.

"It fell out of James's backpack when he knocked it over."

"Why didn't you tell him?"

She glanced around again, checking to make sure that James wasn't coming back. Then she turned the phone on.

"What are you doing?" I said.

"I want to take a look, that's all."

"That's James's property. How would you like it if he went creeping around in your phone?"

She just shrugged. "I have nothing to hide. Besides, all I want to do is see what he's always looking at. And check to see if there are any other girls' numbers in here. Come on, Robyn, tell me you aren't curious."

"I'm not," I said. "Give me that." I grabbed for the phone, but she ducked back out of my way and continued to browse.

"Oh," she said, a surprised look on her face.

"What?"

"I thought you weren't curious."

"I'm not."

"Well, you would be if you saw this."

"Morgan!"

"Just take a look, Robyn."

She handed me the phone. There was a photo on the screen—a medium-range shot of a bearded, heavyset man in scruffy work clothes coming out of a rundown house that was surrounded by trees.

"Keep looking," Morgan said.

I scrolled to the next picture, then the next. All the photos were of the same man. There were five or six shots of him coming out of the house, crossing the yard to a battered pickup truck, and getting inside. There was a second series of the same man getting out of the truck in front of what looked like a hardware store, going into the store, coming out again, loading stuff into the bed of the truck, and then getting back inside.

"See the store in the corner of that picture?" Morgan said. She pointed to the screen. "I know where it is. It's in Harris." Harris was a town on the way to Morgan's family's summer home up north.

"Is it just me, or do those look like creepy stalker pictures?" Morgan said.

James had certainly picked an unusual subject for his pictures, but . . . "Maybe he's into photography," I said. "Maybe he's working on some kind of project."

"Please! If he were into photography, he'd be taking pictures with a proper camera, not his phone. Besides, those pictures aren't exactly art."

"You're impossible, Morgan. First you try to convince me that James is the perfect guy for me. Now you're trying to tell me he's a stalker." I began browsing through the phone again.

"I thought you said that was his personal property," Morgan said.

"I'm just looking to see if he has his home number in here so that I can call him and tell him he dropped his phone." But he didn't. He hadn't stored any phone numbers at all. In the end, I decided to leave the phone on in case he tried to track it down by calling his own number. Failing that, I would return the phone at school the next day.

Morgan and I went back to my dad's place and made ourselves something to eat. Then we did our homework. Well, I did my homework. Morgan talked on the phone to Billy for an hour. I tried to remember the last time I had talked to Nick for more than ten minutes. I couldn't wait until the next night. We'd be together at the party. We'd have fun for the first time in ages.

My mom called to see how I was and to deliver a message: "I'm expecting you for dinner tomorrow night."

"I already have plans, Mom."

"This is important, Robyn. I haven't seen you all week. And I have to go out of town on Saturday."

"So, I'll see you when you get back."

"You'll see me tomorrow night for dinner."

"Mom, I'm going to a party. I already accepted the invitation."

"You can go to the party after dinner."

"But—"

"It's called compromise, Robyn. You do what I want—have dinner with me. Then you do what you want—go to your party. Deal?"

As if I had a choice.

I called Nick and left a message telling him that I'd have to meet him at the party and that he should let me know where it was being held.

. . .

The first thing I did when I got to school the next morning was show James the phone that Morgan had picked up in the library.

"Is it yours?" I said. "I found it under the table after you left."

James's face flooded with relief. "I thought I'd lost it," he said. "My dad would have killed me."

"Did you ask him about those pictures?" Morgan said at lunch.

"Right," I said. "And let him know that I peeked into something that's none of my business."

"He took a lot of pictures of the same person, Robyn—a guy who isn't even good-looking."

"Maybe he's a relative or an old friend."

"Maybe if we started a conversation with him about photography..."

"No," I said.

"It's bad enough we even looked through it, Morgan. We are not going to pry. It's none of our business."

CHAPTER **SEVEN**

After school I went home to change. Then I took the bus uptown to the condo building where Ted lived.

Ted beamed at me when he opened the door. He is nowhere near as big and boisterous and good-looking as my father. In fact, he's on the short side—in heels, my mom is easily the taller of the two. He's also mostly bald and can't see much of anything without his glasses. But he's a terrific cook, has an encyclopedic knowledge of jazz, and is incredibly successful in his work. He's a financial analyst—whatever that is. My mom's crazy about him. I don't think it's a coincidence that she picked someone who is home every night and all weekend and who is always more than happy to pamper her when she's had a rough day at the office or in court. My dad never did that. He was hardly ever home.

"Come in, come in," Ted said. "Your mother is in the living room. Dinner will be ready in fifteen minutes."

My mom was on the sofa with her feet curled up under her. She was sipping a glass of wine and looking surprisingly relaxed for a workaholic who was about to get married.

"Robyn, I feel as if I haven't seen you in months," she said, thrusting out her arms. We hugged, and I sat down beside her. Ted bustled in with a plate of canapés—tiny mushroom tarts and miniature triangles of toast topped with slivers of smoked salmon—and a ginger ale for me.

"Join us, Ted," my mother said.

But Ted wouldn't hear of it.

"You two catch up," he said. "I'll crew the galley."

Ted was a sailing fanatic—or had been when he was younger. He kept saying that one of these days he was going to buy a boat, and he and my mother were going to sail around the world. My mom always smiled sweetly, but she never did anything to encourage him. She was uncomfortable at the thought of being surrounded by thousands of miles of open water, especially if there was the slightest chance that the water might be shark-infested.

"So how come you're going out of town, Mom?" I said.

My mom smiled mysteriously.

"I can't tell you yet," she said. "I don't want to jinx anything."

"Are you scouting out honeymoon locations?"

Her smile broadened. My mom never looked happier than when she was with Ted. He seemed to have the opposite effect on her that my dad did.

"How long are you going to be gone?" I said.

"Probably most of the week." There was that smile again. What was going on?

"Is Ted going with you?"

"He's planning to join me for a few days."

"Dinner's ready," Ted called from the kitchen.

My mom continued to smile as she got up off the sofa and swept into the dining room.

Dinner was amazing—grilled fish, baby potatoes, salad, and my all-time favorite—crème brûlée. While we ate, my mother gave me a progress report on the renovations to our house and on her wedding plans.

Finally, over dessert, Ted said, "How about you, Robyn? How's school?"

"Okay, I guess. I'm tutoring a new kid. He's in my homeroom."

"Oh?" my mom said. "Is he cute?"

"Morgan drools every time she sees him," I said.

"And what about you?"

"He's okay, I guess. But—"

"You're stuck on Nick, right?" Ted smiled at me. If I liked Nick, that was fine with him. Ted always made me feel like my happiness was important to him.

I nodded, avoiding the less-than-thrilled look on my mom's face. "I really have to get going, Mom. I don't want to be late."

"You're going to that party with Nick, aren't you?" she said, no longer as cheerful as she had been. "I think it would be a good idea if you came and stayed here with Ted and me." In other words, where I would be farther away from Nick.

"I'm fine where I am, Mom." I folded my napkin—linen, of course. "Dinner was great, Ted. One of these days you're going to have to teach me to make crème brûlée."

"It would be my pleasure," Ted said.

"I mean it, Robyn," my mom said. "I'd feel more comfortable if you were staying here."

I stood up, circled the table, and kissed her lightly on the cheek.

"Have a great trip, Mom. I'll see you when you get back."

"Robyn—"

"Bye, Ted."

I was glad to be out the door and down the elevator. I caught a bus back downtown and then another one to the address that Nick had given me.

. . .

The party was being held in an apartment building where one of Nick's classmates lived. I could hear music pulsing as I made my way down the hall. My stomach fluttered. Nick knew some of my friends, but I really didn't know any of his. So far that hadn't mattered. But after my visit to his school earlier in the week, and the way his classmates had acted around me, I felt self-conscious. I wished that I had asked Nick to meet me so that I could walk in holding his hand instead of arriving all alone.

I paused at the door to the party room and drew in a deep breath. What if Nick wasn't here yet? What if I walked in and no one talked to me?

"Excuse me," a voice said behind me. It was Jenn, the girl who had ignored me the whole time I'd been at the restaurant with Nick. She reached past me and pulled the door open. "You coming in or what?" she said.

I followed her inside.

The pulsing music was much louder now. Everyone stood clustered in the middle of the room. At first all I saw were the backs of the kids closest to me and, at intervals, the faces of the kids farthest from me. They seemed to have formed a large circle. I glanced at Jenn. She grinned at me and walked toward the circle. I followed her.

When I got close enough to get a good look at what was happening, my jaw dropped. Nick was in the middle of the circle with Danny. They were dancing. Not only that, they were good together. They really seemed to know what they were doing, which told me that they'd danced together before. I stared at them. I had never danced with Nick. I had never even suspected that he liked to dance. But there he was, moving to the beat—and to Danny—like it was the most natural thing in the world to him. Everyone around was urging them on. Danny was wearing a short, low-cut dress and spiky heels. Nick, as usual, was dressed completely in black.

Finally the music stopped.

The spectators burst into applause.

Danny pulled Nick close and went up on tiptoes to kiss his cheek. Nick smiled and blushed—something he rarely did.

Then he spotted me.

He said something to Danny, squeezed her hand, and then came through the circle toward me.

"I was worried you got lost or something," he said.

"So I see." The words popped out of my mouth without my thinking. I regretted them as soon as I saw the annoyed look on Nick's face.

"Danny loves to dance," he said. "She's been taking lessons ever since she was a kid. She used to make me practice with her. I hated it."

"It didn't look to me like you were having a terrible time," I said. Even I could hear how snotty I sounded, but I couldn't help myself. I was furious with Danny. And with Nick. Had he even told her that he was seeing me?

Nick took me by the elbow and pulled me aside.

"What's the matter with you, Robyn? I told you that Danny is an old friend. Do you think I'd act the way you're acting if I saw you and Billy dancing?"

"Billy would never kiss me," I said.

"Billy's not a girl." He drew in a deep breath, struggling to control his temper. "Come on. There are people here you haven't met yet."

He took my hand, led me around the room, and introduced me to a dozen or more of his friends. There were so many names that I forgot most of them almost immediately.

A fast song ended, and a slow one began.

"You want to dance?" Nick said.

I looked up at him and nodded. He escorted me onto the dance floor and put his arms around me. We swayed to the music. It was heavenly. I forgot all about Danny.

The slow song was followed by something faster.

"Hey, Nick," Danny said, her eyes twinkling. "Remember this one?"

Nick's cheeks flushed. He shook his head.

"Come on, Nick," someone called. "Show us some more moves."

Someone else nudged him toward Danny. Nick glanced at me. Danny tugged on his hand. She started to sway to the music. People began to clap. She grinned at Nick, and suddenly they were dancing again. I watched enviously. I was nowhere near as good as Danny. And they seemed to be having a great time. Another pulsingly fast song followed, and they kept dancing.

"Those two are amazing together," a girl said.

I turned to look at her, but my eyes met Jenn's instead. She smirked at me.

When the music stopped, Nick and Danny made their way over to where I was standing. She greeted me warmly.

"Bet you didn't know Nicky had so many moves," she said, laughing. "He always told me he wasn't going to practice with me, dancing is for girls. But he's good, right?"

Danny stuck close to him all night. Even though she didn't go to his school, she seemed to have no trouble fitting in. She knew everyone, and everyone knew her. She laughed and joked around and didn't appear to be remotely uncomfortable. I had never seen Nick look so relaxed—and that made me jealous too.

A guy I didn't know came up to me and said hi. Nick introduced him: Devlin. Devlin looked me over and asked me if I wanted to dance.

"Uh, thanks, but—"

"Go ahead," Nick said. "Have some fun."

"But—"

Nick took me aside and whispered in my ear, "These are my friends, Robyn."

"I know."

"So you could at least try to be nice to them."

"I am trying."

"Well, try harder. Loosen up. Have some fun, okay?" His words stung.

"Okay." I smiled at Devlin. "I'd love to dance," I said.

I followed him onto the dance floor. His style of dancing consisted of shuffling his feet and waving his arms—until the fast music ended and the slow music began. Then he wrapped his arms tightly—too tightly—around me and started to move to the beat. I couldn't wait for the music to stop. I thanked him and fled.

I didn't see Nick anywhere.

The back door to the party room was open, and half the guests had spilled out onto a terrace where the air was cooler. I found Nick standing at the railing with Danny, looking out over the city.

"—worried about him," he was saying.

"If he's catching up on his high school stuff, that's good," Danny said. "And he's a father now. That changes people. Joey's not a bad guy, Nick. He always looked out for you, didn't he? I bet he can't wait to get out of there and look after Jack."

"But he's got another two years, minimum," Nick said. "That doesn't seem like a long time, but it's different when you're locked up. A day can seem like a month, and a year can drag by like a century. I'm afraid he'll lose heart and do something stupid."

"That's why your messages are so important. And he's writing back, right?"

I stared open-mouthed at the two of them. Nick was telling Danny things that he had never told me.

"Keep writing him," Danny said. "Keep encouraging him."

Nick nodded and slipped an arm around her. "I didn't realize how much I missed you until I ran into you again. I could always talk to you."

She smiled up at him.

I wheeled around to run back inside and collided with Jenn. She looked at me and then at Nick and Danny.

"Keep up that jealous act and you'll lose him for sure," she sneered.

I shoved past her. Devlin grabbed my hand. I shook it off.

"Hey!" he said, wounded. "Come on, let's dance."

"No," I said, and quickly added an insincere "Thank you." I didn't want to dance with anyone except Nick.

At first Devlin looked hurt. Then he looked angry. He muttered something under his breath. I stormed out of the party room. If Nick wanted to stay with his friends and dance the night away with Danny, he could be my guest.

CHAPTER **EIGHT**

My dad knocked on my bedroom door the next morning. He was wearing the same grungy jeans, work boots, and plaid shirt.

"Did you just get in, Dad?"

"Couple hours ago. I had some paperwork to catch up on. Nick is at the door, Robbie. He wants to talk to you."

I dressed quickly. I felt all jumbled inside. Had he come to apologize for spending so much time with Danny last night? Or was he angry with me?

I couldn't tell by looking at him.

Nick was standing in the door to my dad's loft. He nodded when he saw me, but he didn't smile. That wasn't good. He glanced at my dad, who was working in his office on the far side of the loft. Then he stepped back out into the hall. I went outside with him, and he closed the door so that my dad wouldn't be able to hear us.

"Why did you take off like that last night?" he said. Definitely angry. His eyes burned into me. "I would never have done that to you, Robyn."

It was the worst thing he could have said.

"Really?" I said. "You would never leave without telling me where you were going?"

He glowered at me. He had done exactly that before Christmas last year. He had disappeared for two whole months, and I'd had no idea where he was.

"I apologized for that, Robyn."

"And now you want me to apologize even though you asked me to a party and then spent the whole time with another girl? You didn't even tell me she was going to be there, Nick."

"I didn't know. Leo invited her."

"Who's Leo?"

"It was his party. He invited Danny. He likes her. Everyone does."

"So I noticed."

Nick drew in a deep breath. "You're right," he said.

"I am?"

"I'm sorry I didn't spend more time with you at the party. But there's nothing going on between Danny and me. We're friends. That's it."

He looked so sincere that I couldn't stay mad.

"I'm sorry I left like I did. It's just that . . . she's so pretty. And she's such a great dancer. And . . ." I hesitated. "And you tell her things you never tell me."

He looked surprised. "Like what?"

"About Joey. About how he's doing, what he's doing."

"She knows Joey."

"I know him too."

"Yeah, but you think he's a total screw-up. You don't like him. If they never let him out, you'd be fine with it."

"That's not true."

"Yes, it is, Robyn. I've seen the look on your face when I mention his name."

Okay, so maybe it was true.

"He got you into big trouble, Nick."

"He's my brother."

"He's your stepbrother."

"You think that makes a difference?" Nick said. His nostrils flared. "Joey saved my life. He matters to me. He's always going to matter to me. Danny understands that."

"Danny! I'm tired of hearing about Danny!"

"And I'm getting tired of the way you're acting. It's like a whole side of you that I've never seen before." He shook his head again. "I have to go. I'm meeting someone."

"Don't tell me, let me guess—Danny?"

"As a matter of fact, no. I'm meeting some guys from school. We're working on a project together."

He didn't kiss me. He didn't tell me that he'd see me later. He just turned and started down the stairs. I stood in the hall and listened until his footsteps faded. When I finally went back inside, my dad glanced up from his computer.

"Everything okay, Robbie?"

I nodded. Then I went to my room, closed the door, and burst into tears. I hated the way I was acting, but I hated the way he was acting even more.

. . .

The phone rang and, just like I'd been doing all day, I jumped.

"It's for you, Robbie," my dad called. The slight frown on his face told me that the voice on the other end wasn't one that he recognized, which meant it wasn't Nick.

I took the receiver from him, and he stumbled back to his bedroom. After being up all night, he had spent most of the day sleeping.

"Hello?" I said.

"Robyn, this is Richard Derrick, James Derrick's father. I hope I'm not interrupting anything."

"No, not at all."

"I'm calling to invite you to dinner tomorrow night. I know this is short notice, but I'd love the chance to meet you. James has spoken so highly of you. And I know he'd love some company besides his old dad, especially with such a sad anniversary coming up."

Sad anniversary? I guessed that he was referring to the death of James's mom.

"Well, I—"

"If the weather holds, I thought I'd barbecue. Do you like salmon?"

"Yes," I said. "But—"

"I know it would mean a lot to James if you would come." If that was true, why hadn't James asked me himself? "How about it?"

"Well, I guess I could—"

"Wonderful," James's father said. "Let me give you the address."

CHAPTER **NINE**

Sunday started out bright and sunny, but I felt nothing but gloom. I didn't hear from Nick. I wondered what he was doing and who he was with. I picked up the phone a dozen times to try his number. But every time I did, I thought of Danny. By the time I left my dad's place the weather had changed to match my mood. Clouds had started to gather, and the sky turned from blue to grey. When I got off the bus in James's neighborhood, it was completely overcast.

I found his house with no trouble. His car wasn't in the driveway, but a red Honda was. I walked up onto the front porch and rang the bell. I was not at all prepared for the man who greeted me. He had piercing blue eyes, and he smiled at me as if he were expecting me. James's father. One side of his face was badly scarred, as if it had been hideously smashed, and he leaned heavily on a cane when he opened the door for me.

"You must be Robyn," he said, his voice hearty and booming. "James has told me so much about you. Come in, come in. He should be back any minute."

As he ushered me into the small but immaculate house, I watched his rolling, lopsided gait. If it weren't for the cane, he might have toppled over.

"Please, come on through," he said.

I followed him into the kitchen.

"Sit down," he said. "Can I offer you some lemonade?"

I accepted. He poured me a glass and then perched on a stool at the counter, his cane propped against the cabinets, to cut vegetables for a salad.

"Can I help you with that?" I said.

"No, thanks. I'm fine," he said. "You just relax. Tell me, how is James responding to your tutoring?"

"He's trying hard," I said, which was mostly true.

His dad looked skeptical. "But is he learning?"

"We've only met a few times. But when he concentrates, he does well."

"When he concentrates," Mr. Derrick said. He shook his head. "James has always had problems with that. When I send him to the store for something, I make him repeat what he's supposed to get. Otherwise he forgets. If I give him a list, chances are he'll lose it." He laughed. "Thank God for cell phones." His face grew more serious. "Though James has had other things on his mind for the past little while," he said. "His mother died, you know."

"He told me. I'm sorry."

Mr. Derrick sighed. "We've had our share of family tragedy, that's for sure. It's been hard on both of us, but I think it's been harder for James." He paused and looked at me. "Did he tell you about how he got that limp?"

"He said he'd been in an accident."

"Accident," Derrick said. He gave the word an odd inflection and paused again, as if he were deciding what to say or whether to say anything at all. "In the end, the police logged it as an accident. It happened last year—almost exactly two years after James's mother died. Did he tell you?"

"No."

"It's probably not something that you should discuss with James," Mr. Derrick said. "It would only upset him. But since you're tutoring him, well, maybe you should understand a little about him. He's been through a lot. And after his mother died . . ." He sighed. "I was in the car with James. I don't blame him, of course. He wasn't himself after everything that had happened. James was very close to his mother."

What did he mean, he didn't blame James? Had James crashed the car on purpose? Why would he do something like that? I looked at Mr. Derrick's cane and at his badly scarred face. Had that happened in the same crash?

I heard a car engine outside.

Derrick grabbed his cane and stood up. "That must be James. Come on. Let's surprise him."

We reached the front porch just as James was getting

out of his car. He had a piece of paper in his hand and seemed to be studying it.

His dad called his name.

James jumped. He threw the piece of paper into the front seat of the car, slammed the door, and spun around. His eyes went to me.

"Look who I invited for dinner," his dad said.

James stared at me, processing the fact of my presence.

"Surprise," I said, smiling even though I felt like the last person on earth he wanted to see.

"Well, what do you say, Dee?" his father said.

Dee?

James mumbled a hello. Suddenly I wished I hadn't come. It was obvious I was making James uncomfortable.

"I'm just about ready to put the salmon on the barbecue," Mr. Derrick said. "Why don't you each grab a glass of lemonade and come out and sit on the deck?"

James and I made ourselves comfortable on thickly padded chairs under a large umbrella. As Mr. Derrick lit the barbecue and set foil-wrapped packets of vegetables on the grill, the clouds grew darker and darker overhead. A cool breeze started to blow.

"Feel that?" Derrick said. "We're going to get some rain."

While he worked, I looked around. The backyard was narrow but deep and well landscaped with flower beds and rock gardens. There was even a pond with water lilies floating on it.

"This place must be gorgeous in summer," I said.

"It is," Derrick said. "I wish I could take credit, but the previous owners did all the work. The real estate agent assured me that all of the plants and flowers are perennials, so they don't need much care."

"A good thing, too," James said. He still seemed dazed by my presence. "My dad teases me about forgetting things, but he's the poster boy for absentminded professors."

I looked at Mr. Derrick. "You're a professor?"

He nodded. "I took a leave for a while. During the time off, I wrote a book."

"He means another book," James said. "He's written a dozen of them."

Mr. Derrick smiled. "I'm also searching around for a position. I'd like to ease back into the classroom."

I asked about his book.

"It's hardly a scholarly treatise," he said with a laugh. "In fact, it's a complete departure for me."

"It's a history of everyday things," James said.

"My publisher refers to it as *Everything You Didn't Know You Wanted to Know about Almost Everything*," Derrick said.

"He's not kidding," James said. "Did you know that the first vending machines were invented in 215 B.C.?"

"No way," I said. I glanced at his father for confirmation.

"James is right," Mr. Derrick said. "The inventor was a man named Hero of Alexander. A person inserted a coin into his machine, and it dispensed holy water. Unfortunately, the machine couldn't tell a real coin from a fake one. That problem wasn't solved until considerably later—the 1880s, in fact. The first commercially successful machines made their appearance in London, England. They dispensed postcards . . ."

By the time Derrick put the salmon steaks on to grill, I was convinced that he must be a highly entertaining professor. Not only did he know a lot, he had a real knack for making even the most ordinary things seem fascinating.

I asked if there was anything I could do to help, but he told me that my job as a guest was to relax. When I insisted on doing something, he sent me inside with James to set the table.

"I should wash up," I said to James when we were finished. He directed me to the bathroom, upstairs to the left.

As I headed up the stairs, I heard Mr. Derrick say, "Pour some more lemonade for everyone, Dee. And then come out here and give me a hand."

After I'd finished in the bathroom, I took a quick look around. I felt kind of guilty peeking into rooms, but the doors were open, and my dad always said you could learn a lot about people from the stuff they surrounded themselves with.

The first impression I had of Mr. Derrick was confirmed by a quick glance around. The second floor of the house was as immaculate as the first. James's room, small but bright, was at the top of the stairs, looking out over the back of the house. It was sparsely furnished with only a bed, a desk, a bookshelf, and a wooden trunk—not much stuff at all. I wondered what my dad would have made of that. The walls were completely bare. Maybe James hadn't had time to decorate yet.

The middle room was obviously his dad's study. It contained an enormous desk, a computer, dozens of shelves stuffed with books, and piles of cardboard boxes waiting to be unpacked.

The front bedroom, which I glimpsed from the hall, was as Spartan as James's room except for one thing: there were photographs on one wall. Curious, I crept to the door to take a closer look. Several large, framed photographs showed a boy—the same boy—at various ages, from very young right up to the age of nine or ten. At first I thought they were photos of James. But a quick examination proved me wrong. The boy in the photos resembled James, but where James had hazel eyes, this boy's eyes were clear blue, like Mr. Derrick's. His chin was different too—more pointed than James's. Did James have a brother? Where was he now? And why weren't there any pictures of James in his dad's room? Come to think of it, there weren't any pictures of James anywhere in the house—or of his mother. Were they too painful for James and his father to look at?

Down below, the back door opened and closed again, and I heard low but angry voices.

". . . I just want to get it over with," James was saying.

Get what over with? Dinner? It was obvious that James had been taken aback by my presence. Was he wishing that I wasn't here?

"This isn't the time or place for that conversation," his dad said sharply.

"But—"

"You'll do what needs to be done, Dee. We both will."

I coughed before I started back down the stairs so that James and his dad would know I was coming. But I was drowned out by a deafening thunderclap. A moment later, the sky opened and it began to pour.

"The food," Mr. Derrick wailed.

I started down the stairs and arrived in the kitchen just in time to see James, soaking wet, dash back into the house with the foil-wrapped vegetables and salmon steaks. He set them down on the table and peeled off his sodden T-shirt. Even from where I was standing, I couldn't help but stare. A huge scar ran diagonally across his back, deep reddish-purple. Then I heard his father's voice, hard and sharp.

"I told you I never wanted to see that thing again," he snarled. "It's bad enough that he's dead and that it's your fault—you don't have to flaunt that thing. Go and put a shirt on."

Dead? Who was dead—the boy in the pictures upstairs? And what did Mr. Derrick mean when he said that it was James's fault? What had James done?

James turned to leave the room. He paused when he saw me. His face was red. I don't know whether he suspected I'd overheard his dad or not. As he pushed by me, I got a clear look at a tattoo on his upper left bicep. It was an airplane with a single word—a name—in the middle of it: Greg. James looked back and saw me staring at it. His eyes hardened, and he ran upstairs.

I wished I could go home. Instead, I went back into the kitchen and asked if there was anything I could do.

"Everything seems to be under control," Derrick said in an eerily calm voice. "James rescued our food from the barbecue. Please, have a seat. We'll eat as soon as he gets into some dry clothes."

James returned a few moments later in fresh jeans and a dry T-shirt. The tattoo was hidden under his sleeve. He and his dad glowered at each other for a moment, and the meal got off to an awkward start. I tried the salmon and the vegetables and exclaimed how good they were. James's dad turned his disapproving eyes from James and thanked me, but it seemed as though he was forcing himself to be a gracious host. He began to tell us both about the importance of fish and how it, more than anything else, had led to the colonization of North America and the opening up of the New World. I listened with interest, but James was quiet through the whole meal.

After dessert—an excellent raspberry torte that Mr. Derrick had made—and more conversation, I said that I should be getting home. James surprised me by offering to drive me. I thanked Mr. Derrick for dinner and said goodbye. James was already on the front porch. It had stopped raining. He used his remote to unlock the car doors.

"Dee!" his dad called from inside the house.

James sighed loudly.

"I'll just be a minute," he said. "You can wait for me in the car."

I went out to the driveway and got in the car. As I settled in, I glanced at the piece of paper that James had thrown onto the driver's seat when he'd arrived. A drawing of some kind? I picked it up and looked more closely. It wasn't a drawing after all. It was a map—of one of the largest cemeteries in the city. Someone had drawn an X through one section of the map and, underneath, had written, "Plot XI, Lot 333." I wondered who was buried there. James's mom, maybe. But why would he need a map to find her grave? And why had he thrown the map into the car when his dad and I surprised him at the door?

I heard the front door slam and looked up to see James coming down the porch steps carrying a brown paper bag. I put the map facedown on the driver's seat. James opened the door, picked up the map, and tucked it into the back pocket of his jeans. He handed me the bag.

"It's a piece of torte," he said. "My dad wants you to take some home."

"Thank him for me," I said.

James turned the key in the ignition. "I'm really sorry, Robyn."

"For what?"

"For my dad. For him calling you and dragging you over here."

"He didn't exactly drag me, James. He invited me, and I accepted."

"Knowing him, he asked you and then refused to take no for an answer."

"I was glad to come, James. I had a good time. Your dad's really interesting. He sure knows a lot."

James backed the car out onto the street, and we drove in silence for a while. He seemed lost in his thoughts.

"Is everything okay?" I said finally.

"Yeah." His voice was flat. "Why?"

"I don't know. You seem preoccupied."

"I'm fine. Really."

This was followed by more silence. It stayed that way until we pulled up outside my dad's building.

"Thanks for coming," James said. "And thanks for being so nice to my dad. I think he enjoyed having someone around to listen to his stories. It'll be good for him to get back in front of a classroom. He's at his best when he has an audience."

I wondered if I should ask him about the photographs of the boy that I had seen in his dad's room. Or about the tattoo that had made his dad so angry. No, I decided. It was none of my business. If James wanted to tell me about those pictures or about what had happened to his family, I should let him do it in his way, in his own time.

I reached for the door.

"I really did have a good time, James," I said.

He smiled at me, but it seemed forced. As soon as I climbed out of the car, he squealed away from the curb. I stared helplessly after him.

I stopped on my way up to my dad's loft and knocked on Nick's door. Orion barked in response, but no one answered.

.   .   .

Morgan looked surprised when I met her at her locker the next day after school. I'd just offered to go with her to the pet store so that she could buy some treats for her dog, Missy.

"Aren't you supposed to be tutoring James this afternoon?" she said.

"He blew me off. Is there something wrong with me, Morgan? I feel like I'm being punished. First Nick keeps saying that he's too busy to see me, but he always has plenty of time for Danny. Then James asks me to tutor him because he says he wants to do well this year, but he's been avoiding me all day—and he didn't seem too thrilled when I showed up at his house for dinner yesterday." Was I the problem? Or was it something else? I'd been hoping he might open up to me a little after our tutoring session.

"Maybe he's embarrassed that his dad invited you," Morgan said. "Or . . ." She hesitated.

"What?" I said.

"Maybe he likes you, but he doesn't know how to deal with it because he knows you have a boyfriend."

"Maybe have a boyfriend," I said gloomily. "Wait, what do you mean, he knows I have a boyfriend? I never told him that."

"No, but Billy did."

"He did? When? Why?"

"It happened sometime last week," Morgan said. "But Billy didn't tell me about it until the weekend. James asked about you, and Billy told him that you were seeing someone. That was what you wanted him to say, right? I mean, you don't want James chasing after someone who isn't available, do you? Besides, Britt Anderson has been making eyes at him."

"She has?" Britt was in my French class. Guys drooled over her because she was super attractive, with pouty lips and perky breasts and a reputation for, well, knowing how to have a good time.

"I saw her talking to James in the library during my spare," Morgan said. "I told you, Robyn. He's cute. And that shy thing really works for him. It makes him seem vulnerable. It was only a matter of time before someone decided to sweep him up."

"Great," I muttered.

"I thought you weren't interested."

"I'm not." At least, I didn't think I was. "It's just that everyone seems to have someone—except me."

We walked down to a downtown shopping street

and headed for the pet store. We were about to go inside when I stopped short.

"Maybe you got it backwards," I said. "Maybe Britt wasn't hitting on James. Maybe it was the other way around—he was hitting on her." And maybe that was why James had been less than enthusiastic about my presence at dinner. Maybe he'd been wishing Britt was there instead.

Morgan frowned. "Why? What makes you—" She turned to look where I was looking. "Oh," she said.

James was coming out of a florist's shop a few doors down from the pet store. He was carrying flowers.

"Well, they're not for Britt," Morgan said, "unless she's into the whole Goth thing and no one told me."

"What do you mean?" I said.

"Look."

I looked. Then I turned back to her. "I don't—"

"Those aren't date-type flowers, Robyn—unless you're dating a vampire. Calla lilies and white roses? That's something you'd see at a funeral."

Or on a grave. I stared at Morgan for a moment. Then I turned and watched James get into his car and drive away.

. . .

There were dozens of things I could have done after Morgan and I split up. I could have gone home and done my homework. I could have cleaned up my room. I could have stopped by Nick's place to see if he was home. I could have gone for a run to let off some steam—and I seriously needed to let off steam.

Maybe Morgan was right. Maybe Nick wasn't the best person for me. But if that were true, why was I so miserable whenever I thought about losing him? Or maybe that was Morgan's point. Maybe when you really cared about another person, it wasn't supposed to make you miserable and afraid. Besides, if I cared so much about Nick, why was I thinking about James? Why wasn't I tracking Nick down and trying to have a heart-to-heart with him? Why had I decided to go looking for James instead?

If Morgan was right about those flowers, then I had a pretty good idea where James had gone—the cemetery, the one he had a map for. A map that, for some reason, he hadn't wanted his father to see. Maybe James was acting the way he was because of whoever was buried in Plot XI, Lot 333. Maybe it had something to do with what his dad had said to him yesterday. Maybe he needed someone to talk to. Maybe I could help.

It took me two buses and forty-five minutes to get to the cemetery—which turned out to be even larger than I had expected. Just inside the cemetery gates, on a large display board, was a full-color version of the map that I had seen in James's car. Plot XI was on the far side of the cemetery, down a path in what turned out to be a lovely green valley. Lot 333 was tucked away against a hedge. I recognized it instantly by the fresh calla lilies and white roses that had been set into a metal vase in front of the headstone. I looked around. No sign of James. I approached the stone and read the name on it: Gregory Paul Johnson.

Greg—like the tattoo on James's arm.

I looked at the dates on the tombstone. Gregory Johnson had been nine years old when he died—exactly five years ago. I thought about the photos I had seen in Mr. Derrick's room. That boy looked about nine. Were they pictures of Gregory Johnson? Who was he? What role had James played in his death? And why did that name sound vaguely familiar?

. . .

"Have you guys seen James today?" I asked Morgan and Billy when I caught up with them the next day at lunch. "He wasn't in homeroom this morning."

"I haven't seen him," Billy said.

"Maybe he's sick," Morgan said.

"Maybe." But I was pretty sure he wasn't. He had been at the cemetery yesterday, delivering flowers on the fifth anniversary of the death of a nine-year-old boy—a boy whose death James might have been involved in. "I think I'll go by his place after school and see how he is."

"Good idea," Morgan said, winking at me. "Get over there before you-know-who gets her claws into him."

I thought about telling her that wasn't the reason I wanted to check up on him. I also thought—not for the first time—about telling her what I had seen and overheard at James's house. Usually I let Morgan in on everything. But something stopped me. James was so shy, so vulnerable, and so obviously unhappy. It just didn't seem right to be saying things about him when, really, I had no idea what was going on. Given how Morgan had reacted to the pictures in James's phone, I decided to keep my mouth shut. I would respect James's privacy and get my facts straight before I said a word.

· · ·

It was a warm afternoon, and the windows of the Derrick house were open, which was how I heard Mr. Derrick before I even got to the porch.

"Pull yourself together, Dee," he said. "I'm counting on you. Your brother is counting on you."

Brother? Those pictures I had seen in Mr. Derrick's room . . .

"You can't mess up this time, Dee. This is your last chance. It has to be done right."

"It will be," James said. "I did exactly what you told me to do. I know where to find him. That's the most important part, isn't it?"

Where to find who? Was he still talking about Gregory Johnson and the cemetery? I thought about the strange pictures that Morgan and I had found in James's cell phone.

"The most important part is that you get it right this time," Mr. Derrick said. "That you focus. Concentrate. Remember every single thing I told you. The most important thing is that you don't let me down this time, that you don't let Greg and your mother down—again."

"I won't let them down," James said. He sounded upset. "I told you that, didn't I? I promised."

I backed away from the porch steps. Maybe this wasn't the best time to drop by. Maybe—

The front door flew open, and James burst out. He stopped dead in his tracks when he saw me. Then he thumped down the steps and ran past me.

"James, wait!" I said.

He was at the car already and was opening the door. "James!"

He paused and looked evenly at me. "What?" he said. "What are you doing here?"

"You weren't in school today. I was worried."

"Worried? Worried about what?" He was angry now. Once again, I wished I hadn't come to this house.

"You skipped tutoring yesterday."

"I told you, I had something to do. God, I wish everybody would just get off my back!" His eyes shifted from me to the house behind me. I turned and saw Mr. Derrick framed in the living room window.

"Come on," James said. "I'll take you home."

He kept his eyes steady on his father as he turned the key in the ignition and backed out of the driveway. He drove in silence for a few blocks before pulling over to the curb and killing the engine. It took a few moments before he turned to face me.

"Yesterday was a kind of anniversary for me," he said. "But not the anniversary of anything good."

Even though I already knew what he was talking about, I held my tongue. There were some things that you just couldn't force.

"My little brother died five years ago," he said.

"I'm sorry," I murmured.

James stared out the windshield.

"What happened?" I asked.

James still didn't look at me. "He was murdered."

CHAPTER **TEN**

James was silent for a few moments. So was I. Gregory Johnson, nine years old, had died five years ago. James had the name Greg tattooed onto his arm. His father had just warned him that he couldn't let Greg down again. It didn't make perfect sense, but Gregory Johnson seemed to be James's brother.

"Are you busy right now?" James said.

"Well, I—"

"I'd like to show you something." His eyes burned into mine. "It won't take long. I promise."

. . .

We drove to a place that I had visited for the first time only one day earlier. James pulled the car over to the side of the road and sat for a moment, gripping the steering wheel. I gazed at the fence and the expanse of lawn and trees beyond. It looked like a beautiful, well-kept park—if you ignored the headstones standing in rows under the shade of stately trees.

James stared out through the windshield. After a few moments, he drew in a deep breath and got out of the car. I scrambled after him and followed him through the gate and into the cemetery.

We walked in silence, James's face rigid, his limp pronounced—as I realized it was whenever he was tired or upset. We followed a different path from the one I had taken earlier. This one wound its way through what looked like the oldest part of the cemetery—I glanced at dates on headstones and mausoleums as we walked—and then slowly downward into the familiar valley and back toward the thick hedge. James stopped in front of Gregory Paul Johnson's headstone and bowed his head.

"I know you saw the tattoo," he said quietly.

"James, I didn't mean—"

He pushed up his sleeve and showed me his left arm.

"My dad hates it. He'd burn it off if he could."

I didn't know what to say.

"You heard what he said to me, didn't you?" he said. "You heard him say it was my fault."

"I didn't mean to eavesdrop," I murmured.

"The way my dad yells, you'd have to be deaf not to hear him." He reached out and touched the letters that had been carved deep into the stone. "Greg was my brother. He was shot."

Shot?

"It was my fault."

I stared first at the stone and then at the anguished expression on James's face. What did he mean? Surely he hadn't shot his own brother.

"What happened, James?"

James traced the letters of his brother's name one by one.

"The night it happened, our dad took us to a movie," he said finally. "Greg really loved seeing movies. He liked to go to the theater where there were other people. Lots of other people. He liked the comfortable seats and the smell of popcorn and the darkness in the theater. My dad took him to every kids' movie that came out.

"Dad couldn't find a parking space close to the movie theater. He finally left the car in an alley. He said it would be safe there and that he wouldn't get a ticket. When we got out of the movie, we walked back to where the car was. My dad wanted to stop and get cigarettes. He used to smoke. Greg was totally hyper from the movie and from the candy my dad had let him eat, even though my mom kept telling him too much candy wasn't a good idea. Greg could get really excited, you know? He was running all over the place, so my dad told me to go on ahead with Greg, you know, so Greg wouldn't act up in the store. He said to wait for him in the car. He gave me the keys."

He stared at the stone, his head bowed slightly.

"It was my job to watch out for Greg. It was always my job to watch out for him, because I'm older—I was older." He looked up at me. "We moved to this place out in the suburbs right after Mom married my dad. My real dad died when I was a baby. Mom married Richard. She had Greg when I was three."

"So he's your half-brother," I said.

"He was my brother," James said fiercely. Nick had reacted the same way when I'd called Joey his stepbrother. "My mom told me that a million times. Maybe we had different dads, but he was my brother. And he was younger, so it was my job to look after him. And I did. I always did my best. But—"

Suddenly I wished that I hadn't come with him. I wished I didn't have to see the look of anguish on his face or hear the grief in his voice.

"There was a creek out behind our house. In the spring, when the snow was melting or when there was a big rain, the creek would swell and the water would run really fast. We weren't supposed to go near it when that happened. When we went outside, it was my job to make sure that Greg stayed away from the water." He touched the cold stone again with his fingertips. "I turned my head for a minute. I swear, it was just one minute. Maybe less. I heard Greg scream. I don't know how it happened, but he was in the water, being swept away. I yelled for help. I yelled until I lost my voice. I ran along the creek—but the water was so fast, and I was scared."

He laid his hand flat on his brother's headstone. "There was a neighbor out with his dog. If he hadn't come along when he did, Greg would have drowned. But this man saved him. He brought him out, did CPR on him, and rushed him up to the house. When Richard—my dad—found out what had happened, he hit me. My mother was screaming. She had to pull him off me."

"You must have been terrified," I said.

James stared at the stone.

"I shouldn't have turned my head," he said. "But Greg—" He shook his head. "He could be such a pain. My dad let him do whatever he wanted. Greg could get away with murder, and he knew it. I got in trouble all the time because of him. But he was smart, too. And funny. He could really make me laugh. Whenever my dad got mad at me, Greg would always come up to my room and clown around until he got me to laugh."

He smiled at the thought, but a moment later his smile faded. "Anyway, we moved back to the city again a few years later. The night we went to the movies, my dad went into the store, and Greg and I went across the street to the car. There were all these garbage cans in the alley. They were smelly, and I was afraid there might be rats. I told Greg we should wait on the street. But he was fooling around, and he didn't listen to me. He ran into the alley. I couldn't let him go in there alone. I went in after him to get him. There was a man in the alley. He shot Greg."

He closed his eyes and drew in a deep, shuddery breath.

"Greg was lying on the ground. There was blood all over the front of his shirt, and he had a surprised look on his face, like he couldn't believe what happened. He was looking right at me, trying to say something, but he couldn't get the words out. I ran to where he was and knelt down beside him and held his hand." James swallowed hard. "I held his hand. And he went still and quiet. He died."

A tear trickled down his cheek. He rubbed fiercely at it.

"My dad said he was coming out of the store when he heard a big bang. He said his first thought was that it was a car backfiring. Then he heard me. I was screaming for him. He started to run to where the car was parked. He said other people must have heard, too, because they were moving toward the alley—all except this one man who was hurrying away from the sound instead of toward it. My dad told me later that he should have realized, but that he wasn't thinking."

"Realized?"

"Who the guy was," James said. "He said he wished he had taken a good look at him—if he'd known what was going to happen . . . But by then it was too late."

He pulled his hand away from the headstone.

"I was kneeling on the ground, holding Greg's hand. I remember my dad showing up. I remember him talking to me. Then the cops arrived, and an ambulance, but that part's all kind of a blur. My dad told me later that I wouldn't let go even when the paramedics arrived. He said he had to pry me loose from Greg. The cops were there, too. They kept asking me questions—what did I see, where did the man go, what did he look like? But I just kept seeing Greg lying on the ground, covered in blood, staring up at me with that surprised look on his face."

"Did you see the guy who did it?"

A faraway look came into his eyes.

"He had dark eyes—I couldn't tell what color exactly—a long, thin nose, ears that stuck out, shaggy brown hair, a small mouth, and a scar on his chin, right here." He pointed. "And he had a gun. I got a good look at it. It looked huge. Later—I think at the police station—I told a cop how I had stared at that gun. He must have written down what I said or told someone about it, because it came up at the trial."

He stepped away from the grave and looked down at the ground.

"The cops thought maybe the guy was trying to break into my dad's car or steal it. I described him to them. They showed me some pictures, and I picked him out. Then they showed the pictures around, and they found a man who said he'd seen the same guy in the area maybe a half hour before the movie ended. They found someone else who had seen him even earlier. The cops found the guy and brought him in. They put him in a lineup and asked me if I would see if I recognized him. I was terrified. What if he saw me? What if he had friends who would try to kill me?" He looked sheepishly at me. "Pretty selfish of me, huh?"

"You were just a kid, James."

"I didn't want to do it. I was crying. Can you believe it? My little brother had been shot dead, and I was crying because I was scared of what would happen to me." He shook his head. "If they hadn't let my dad stay with me, I don't think I could have done it." His eyes skipped back to the gravestone.

"I picked him out. He had a record. He had a drug problem, he'd stolen stuff before and had done some muggings, stuff like that. The police arrested him. I remember how happy my parents were when they heard. My dad said they would get him for sure. They said the guy would pay for what he did to Greg. I thought it was all over. But it didn't turn out that way."

"What do you mean?"

"I thought it would be like TV. I thought once they arrested him, they would make him confess. But he didn't confess. Then I thought, okay, so then I'll go to court and tell everyone exactly what had happened, and they'll know he's guilty, and he'll go to prison for the rest of his life. But it wasn't like that. The cops didn't find the guy's fingerprints on the car or even in the alley. They never found the gun that he'd used to shoot Greg. They didn't find any of Greg's blood on the guy's clothes. Basically, it came down to what I had seen. I thought everyone would believe me, but they didn't."

That was no surprise, either. How many times had I heard my parents talk about eyewitness evidence—from opposite sides? They both agreed that eyewitness evidence is the least reliable type of evidence there is. What eyewitness see—or think they see—can be influenced by the weather or lighting or faulty memories. In a case like the one James was describing, where there was only one witness to the actual crime—and where the whole case hinged on what that one witness, a kid, said—a good defense attorney would go after that witness. A good defense attorney would shake that eyewitness up and do his best to get the witness to admit he wasn't one hundred percent positive. It's up to the prosecutor to prove guilt beyond a reasonable doubt. All the defense has to do is create that doubt.

"It took forever until the trial happened," James said. "Months and months." His voice started to quaver.

"James, you don't have to—"

His expression was fierce when he turned to look at me.

"I do," he said. "I do."

I nodded.

"Finally the trial happened," he continued. "The prosecutor explained to me how I should answer the questions—I should be truthful. If I wasn't sure, I should say so. If I needed a minute to think, I should take it. I shouldn't be nervous. And that's what I did when I got to court. The prosecutor asked if the person I'd seen in the alley was in court and I said yes. I pointed to him. My parents were watching me the whole time. My mom looked proud."

I tried to imagine what it must have been like to be Greg Johnson's parents, sitting there in court, watching their other son testify. All those hopes pinned on one boy.

"Then the guy's lawyer started asking questions," James said. "They seemed so easy—what did Greg and I do when the movie was over? Where did I go? Where did he go? What made me go into the alley? The lawyer seemed nice, and I answered the questions. But then . . ."

He looked at the headstone again. "There were more questions. They got more detailed. What did I remember about the person I said I had seen in the alley? Was it light or dark in the alley? How far away was the person I said I had seen? Was it true that I told the police that when I saw the gun, I was scared the guy was going to shoot me? Did I also tell the police that the gun looked huge, bigger than anything I had ever seen? Did I know that according to some expert, the gun that shot Greg was actually a small gun—a .22? Would I like to see how big a .22 actually is?"

His voice grew bitter.

"The way it went," he said, "was that if I was wrong about the gun, then maybe I was wrong about the man I'd seen. Didn't I tell the police that he was really tall? I did. I did say that. But it turned out he was just average. I said I thought he was holding the gun in his right hand, but the guy turned out to be left-handed. The lawyer got me all confused. I could tell by the way the jury was looking at me that they thought I was just some confused kid. I remember that lawyer saying, 'Maybe you made a mistake. If you did, nobody will blame you for that.' After all, my brother was lying on the ground, I was terrified. It was perfectly understandable if I got confused about who I said I had seen. And then, of course, there was no physical evidence."

My dad always says that physical evidence is the best kind of evidence—it never lies, never changes, never makes mistakes. A case with solid physical evidence, he says, is the kind that's most likely to stand up in court.

"You know what happened?" James said. "You want to guess how it turned out?"

CHAPTER ELEVEN

"The guy got off," James said. "He got off. And you know what? When the verdict came in, when they said not guilty, the guy turned and looked right at me. He looked like he wanted to kill me. He came up to me after it was all over—I was really scared. He said because of me, he'd lost his little girl. He said he was going to get me for that."

"What did he mean?"

James shook his head. "I don't know. My dad told me not to listen to him. He took me out of there. But the guy called our house. He said he was going to get me. I had nightmares about him every night."

"That's awful," I said.

"My parents took the verdict hard. My mom said it wasn't my fault, but that didn't stop her from crying and crying. My dad didn't say anything. If my mom or I ever mentioned Greg, he got up and left the room. And school?" He shook his head. "I couldn't stand to go there anymore. I felt like everyone was staring at me, everyone was saying, 'That's the guy who screwed up and let his brother's killer go free.'"

"I'm sure nobody really thought that."

"I should have told them that I wasn't confused. I should have said I knew exactly who killed my brother— I would have recognized him anywhere. He was sitting right there in that courtroom. It was him. We moved after that. We all just wanted to get away. But it didn't help. Six months after we left, my mom died."

Oh.

"It was what they call a 'single-vehicle accident,'" James said. "It happened on a hill near our new house. She smashed into a pole. Car was totaled. The cops said she must have been going 35 miles an hour when she hit that pole. They said there were no skid marks—it looked like she didn't even try to stop."

I felt sick for him. I thought about the so-called accident he and his father had been in. That had happened a year ago—almost exactly two years after James's mother had died, according to his dad. Mr. Derrick had said that he was in the car with James—the way he'd said it, it was obvious that James had been driving. Had James been so filled with guilt that he had tried to end it all? I remembered the scars on his body. I couldn't begin to imagine how he must have felt as tragedy piled up on tragedy. It seemed like far too much for one person to bear.

"Why did you move back here, James?"

"My dad wanted to come back. He thought it would help. And after everything he'd been through . . ."

After everything he'd been through?

"I didn't want to come," James said. "I didn't want to have anything to do with this place or with anyone who knew me. I didn't want to be that kid again—the one who had let his brother's killer walk free. So . . . I changed my name," he said. "My real name is David James Johnson." So that was why his dad called him Dee. "I changed it so no one would know it was me. But you know what? It didn't help. I still know I'm me."

"It's not your fault, James," I said again.

"Then why does it feel like it is? He was my brother, Robyn, and I let him down. I let my parents down too. My mom never recovered. Even before the . . . the accident, she wasn't the same person. She cried every night for Greg. Every night. And my dad blames me for everything."

"I'm sure he doesn't."

James looked deep into my eyes, and in that moment I saw years of grief and regret.

"Yes, he does, Robyn. He does."

. . .

We drove home in silence. I had no idea what to say, and James seemed lost in bitter memories. When he finally pulled up in front of my dad's building, he said, "I'll understand if you don't want to tutor me anymore."

"Of course I want to tutor you," I said. "Why wouldn't I?"

"After everything I told you?"

"I still want to tutor you, James. Really." Did he seriously think that I would drop him over something that he wasn't responsible for? I put a hand over his to reassure him. "We'll get together tomorrow after school, okay?"

The gratitude in his eyes made me feel even sorrier for him.

"Thanks, Robyn," he said. He leaned over and kissed me on the cheek. When I looked at him in surprise, his face turned bright red. "Oh god, I'm sorry. I . . . I just . . ."

"It's okay," I said. "We're friends, aren't we, James?"

He smiled shyly at me. "Friends sounds good."

I opened the car door and started to get out.

"Robyn?"

I turned back to him.

"About what I told you . . . I felt like I owed you an explanation, you know, because of my dad and because you've been so nice to me. But—" There was that anguished look again. "You don't have to tell anyone, do you? Don't get me wrong—I'm not sorry I told you. Okay, maybe a little sorry. I don't want you to think—"

"I don't think anything, James, except that I'm sorry for what you and your family have been through."

That earned me a rueful smile.

"I just don't want everyone at school to be talking about me again. That was supposed to be the whole point. We were supposed to come back here, and my dad was supposed to find a job and I was supposed to finish school. If I can get through this year—and I'm pretty sure I can, with your help—and pick up a few credits during the summer, I can get out of here."

"You mean, leave again?"

"Maybe I can get into college somewhere far from here. It's not that I want to forget Greg. It's just that—"

"It's okay, James," I said. "Your secret is safe with me. Promise. I'll see you tomorrow, okay?"

I slid out of the car and watched him pull away from the curb. It was only after he'd gone that I looked across the street and saw Nick. He was standing in the park with Orion. Danny was with them. Her silver Lexus was parked close by. Nick scowled at me, then turned and jerked on Orion's leash. The three of them walked to Danny's car, and Nick put Orion in the backseat. He got up front with Danny, and they drove away.

Terrific, I thought. Tears welled up in my eyes. I wished Nick had a cell phone so that I could call him and tell him that what he'd seen wasn't what he probably thought he'd seen—assuming that he even cared. I wasn't sure of that anymore.

A tear dribbled down my cheek. I rubbed it away and headed upstairs. There was no one home.

I stood inside the door for a moment, wondering how things had gone so wrong between Nick and me. We'd had such a great summer. Okay, maybe the first half of it had got off to a rocky start. Nick had spent it at a group home for troubled boys, trying to find out what had happened to the brother of an old friend. I'd stayed at Morgan's summerhouse. And true, Nick and I hadn't seen much of each other during the second half. But when he'd come to Morgan's place for a couple of weekends, he had seemed to enjoy my company. He had been sweet and attentive. He'd even gotten along reasonably well with Morgan. I'd thought everything was perfect.

Now I was beginning to wonder. Maybe it hadn't been so perfect. Who knew what Nick had been up to in the city without me? He had run into his old friend Danny, who had landed him a job at her dad's company—and it strangely had never came up that she was a girl—and he and Danny had spent every night together at work. He had reconnected with her parents, and it seemed pretty clear that he was more comfortable around them than he was around my mom and dad. My father had always treated Nick well. But my mom had never been thrilled that I was seeing him. Danny's parents were obviously different. They had known Nick when he was just a kid. They had known his mother, too. They had seen first-hand what Nick's stepfather was like. They knew what he had done—to Nick and to his mom. Maybe that made all the difference. Maybe that was why they were willing to give him the benefit of the doubt. They had started in the same place as Nick and his family. They knew the worst about him, but they didn't hold it against him.

But what did that mean? Sure, Nick and I were different from each other. But were we too different to make it work? Were we too different for Nick to want to make it work? Was Morgan right—was James a better person for me?

When it came right down to it, Morgan didn't know a thing about James. The poor guy. I felt so sorry for him. He'd dealt with so much. But here he was, struggling to get his life on track and to make a future for himself. My problems seemed like nothing compared to his.

I drew in a deep breath and pulled myself up straight. I would talk to Nick in the morning before school. I would apologize for the way I had been behaving. And I would brace myself for whatever he decided to say to me.

I went into my room and sat down at the desk. I pulled my schedule out of my backpack and looked at my homework assignments. With a sigh, I switched on my computer. And then, because it was on anyway, I went online and Googled the name Gregory Paul Johnson. I didn't pull up a lot of information, just a few old news articles. The facts were all pretty much as James had described them. But there was one piece of information he hadn't mentioned. I stared at it, stunned. No wonder Gregory Johnson's name had sounded familiar.

CHAPTER **TWELVE**

"Robyn, I was just going to call you," my mother said when I reached her on her phone. She sounded upbeat, even excited. I guessed that Ted must have already joined her out west.

"How's the trip, Mom?" I said, even though that wasn't the reason I had called.

"It's been great," my mother said. "You're going to love it out here, honey."

"Me? What are you talking about, Mom?"

"I was going to wait until I came home to tell you. But they want an answer soon. Robyn, I've been offered a job out here."

I was so astonished that I couldn't speak.

"Robyn? Are you still there? Did you hear what I said?"

"You're not going to take it, are you, Mom?"

"That's what I wanted to talk to you about. It's a

terrific opportunity for me. Ted arrived today. We're looking at houses."

"Houses? You mean you are going to take it?"

"I haven't given them my answer yet. They're giving me a week to decide. But I don't see how I can pass it up. Ted is willing to relocate. And you really will love it, Robyn. This city's beautiful. The ocean is on one side and the mountains are on the other."

"But I don't want to move." I really didn't. Morgan and Billy were here. My dad was here. Nick was here.

"We can talk about it when I get back," my mom said. She didn't sound nearly as excited. I guess I hadn't responded the way she had hoped. "If you want, you can fly out here on Friday and spend the weekend with Ted and me. You can take a look around."

"I can't," I said. "I have plans." It was an out-and-out lie. I just didn't want to go out there. I didn't want to look around. I didn't want to move.

"Mom, the reason I was calling . . ." I hesitated. I had promised James that I wouldn't tell anyone about him. But there were a few questions I needed answered. "You remember that boy who was shot a few years ago? Gregory Johnson?"

"Yes," my mom said. Her tone was guarded. No surprise there. She had been the lawyer for Edward Leonard, the man who had been charged with the murder. In our house, the case hadn't been referred to as the Gregory Johnson murder trial; it had been known as the Eddy Leonard trial. My parents had been on the verge of separation then, and it was one more thing they argued about—my dad the cop and my mom the criminal defense attorney. For once, I was glad that I had my father's last name instead of my mother's. I could only imagine what James would think if he knew who I really was.

"We're doing a law unit in social studies. We have to do a project." It was another lie, but for a good reason. I could just imagine what my mom would say if she knew that I was tutoring the boy she'd demolished on the witness stand. "I want to do my project on eyewitness evidence. You were the lawyer for the guy they arrested, weren't you?"

"Yes." She sounded even more guarded.

"That case was all about eyewitness evidence, wasn't it?"

"Partly," my mother said. "My client was arrested on the basis of eyewitness identification. But there were other considerations."

"Such as?"

"Can we talk about this another time, Robyn?"

"I just want a little information, that's all, Mom."

I heard her sigh. "There was more to it than the eyewitness account," she said, "although that's the part that everyone seems to remember. I also introduced my client's criminal record into evidence."

"You did? I thought defense lawyers were always trying to have that information excluded."

"Generally they do," she said. "But in this case, it seemed relevant. Edward Leonard—my client—had been convicted of some petty theft, some breaking and entering, but he had never been involved in car theft and had never been known to carry a weapon of any kind. I had police officers testify to this. You remember Charlie Hart, Robyn?"

He was a homicide detective and a friend of my dad's.

"He testified."

"He was involved?"

"He was the arresting officer. Even he had to admit that the incident in question"—I wondered how James would have reacted if he'd heard his brother's murder referred to as an incident—"seemed out of character for Edward Leonard. I don't know if that case is the best example for your assignment," she said. "I can suggest something else if you'd like."

"No, it's okay," I said. "Thanks, Mom."

"Are you sure you can't come out this weekend and look around?"

"Mom, I really don't want to move."

I heard a long sigh on my mother's end of the line.

"We'll talk when I get home," she said.

.   .   .

I love my mother. I really do. But I also know what she can be like. She's not the kind of person to settle. When she does something, she does it all the way. She also takes things—all things—seriously. Especially her job. When she was in law school she was always studying. She'd have a law book propped open on the kitchen counter while she was cooking. Once she started practicing, she spent long hours in her home office, preparing whatever case she was working on. That makes her a good lawyer. At least, that's what people say.

But I had never really thought much about her actual job. She defends people who are accused of breaking the law. Sometimes these people have been accused of serious crimes, like murder. Sometimes, as in the case of James's brother, they have been accused of murdering a child. When that happens, it's my mother's job to do whatever she can to defend her client against the charge. That can mean relentless questioning of a witness to point out any problems with their stories, anything that will create doubt in the minds of the jury. I had never thought much about that, either.

Until now.

It had never occurred to me that there were times, maybe plenty of times, when my mother did her job so well that innocent people ended up getting hurt, the way James had. My mom was always happy when she won her case. It had never occurred to me to consider the other side, the losing side—families and loved ones of the victims who had been hoping their nightmares would end. It had never occurred to me that some people might really have gotten away with murder—thanks to my mother.

James would hate me if he knew who I really was—who my mom was. I felt a heavy lump in my stomach.

Okay, so James had changed his name. He didn't want anyone to know about his past. But it was bound to come out sooner or later who my mother was. And then what?

Should I tell him before he heard it from someone else? What would he think, especially after confiding in me what he was keeping secret from everyone else?

Part of me wanted to confess to James. The other part, a bigger part, wished I had never met him.

．　．　．

Morgan called me soon after I had finished talking to my mother.

"I'm at the mall," she said breathlessly. "You know, to exchange that top I bought last week."

"Uh-huh." I was still thinking about the bombshell my mom had dropped on me. Move? There was no way. I liked it right where I was.

"Robyn, I just saw Nick."

"Congratulations," I said. "Seems like everyone sees more of him than I do. Did you talk to him?"

Silence.

"Morgan?"

"The thing is," Morgan said slowly, "he was kind of kissing another girl."

"Kind of kissing?" I said. "What girl?"

"She was really pretty, Robyn. Tall and thin, with long blonde hair—totally dyed," she added.

"Danny."

I heard a gasp.

"That was Danny? She looks like a supermodel."

Terrific.

Morgan must have realized what she'd said. "What I mean is—"

"She's gorgeous. I know. And Nick was kissing her? You're sure?"

"I know what kissing looks like, Robyn."

"Well, they are friends. They've known each other forever."

"You and Billy are friends," Morgan said. "But if I ever saw you kiss him like that, I'd scratch your eyes out."

I felt sick all over.

"I'm sorry," Morgan said. "I debated whether I should tell you or not. Then I decided that if it were me, I'd want to know."

"Are you sure it was that kind of kiss?"

"Positive. I was coming out of Lulu's, and I saw them at the jewelry store—you know the one I mean. Nick must have bought something, because a clerk gave him a bag. He said something to Danny. And she put her arms around him and kissed him. I mean, she really kissed him, Robyn."

My whole body went numb. The room around me faded to black. Danny had known Nick forever. Everyone at Nick's school treated Nick and Danny as if they were a couple. She saw him more often than I did. She had found him a job—working with her. Her parents didn't seem to have a problem with him.

And now he was kissing her.

"Robyn, I'm sorry," Morgan said.

"Tell me again what you saw," I said.

She repeated the whole story.

"And he let her kiss him like that?" He'd told me there was nothing between them. It had never occurred to me that he might mean it literally.

"I didn't see him resist."

"And you saw the whole thing? From start to finish?"

"You sound like your mom."

"Did you, Morgan?"

"I saw her kiss him." There was a pause.

"What?"

"Well, this idiot who was texting slammed into me. Really hard. I told him off, and when I looked again, Nick and Danny were on their way out of the store."

"So you didn't see the whole thing?"

"Well, no. But Robyn? He had his arm around her—around her shoulder—when they left the store. I'm sorry."

Danny. Why did she have to show up? Why hadn't she stayed wherever she'd been all this time? I hated her. But deep down I knew it wasn't all her fault. Just because she was there, that didn't mean that Nick had to be interested in her. If he really cared about me, she would just be another girl, the way every guy in my school was just another guy to me.

If he really cared.

"Maybe my mother is right," I said. "Maybe I'd like it out west."

"Out west?" Morgan said. "What are you talking about?"

I told her my mother's news.

"No way!" Morgan said. "You can't move. You're my best friend. What would I do without you?"

"I may have no choice, Morgan."

"You have to stay. You can't go. What does your dad say?"

"He doesn't know yet."

"He won't let you go. I know it."

I wasn't sure that he would have more of a choice than I did.

CHAPTER **THIRTEEN**

I set my alarm for extra early and was dressed and sitting on the stairs to the second floor when Nick arrived home from work. He looked surprised to see me. He also looked tired. He stopped a few steps below me and looked up at me.

"What are you doing up so early?" he said.

"I wanted to talk to you—about the way things have been going. We never have time to talk. You're always so busy. I thought maybe you could take a day off this weekend. Maybe we could do something—just the two of us."

I prayed he would say he wanted to be with me. I prayed Morgan had been wrong.

"I have Saturday off," Nick said. His eyes shifted away from me as he spoke.

"Perfect. We can do whatever you want."

"I have Saturday off," he said again, looking at me

115

this time. "But I already made plans."

"What plans?"

"I'm going with Danny to visit a friend of her dad's."

Danny again.

"It's the guy who's the vet," Nick said quickly, maybe because he wanted to explain before I could say anything, or maybe because he was excited about the visit. "I told you about him. He invited me to come out and spend the day, watch what he does, see what the work is like."

"Can't you go another time?"

"I already said yes. Danny's dad set it up, Robyn. He's been really nice to me. Danny's going to drive me. It's out of town."

I guess what I was thinking showed on my face. Nick shook his head again.

"I thought you'd be happy for me, Robyn. I thought you'd be glad I'm thinking about what I want to do with my life. I was going to tell you yesterday when I saw you. But you were too busy kissing that guy."

"It wasn't what you think. It wasn't that kind of kiss."

"Yeah? What kind of kiss was it?"

"He's new at school. He was just grateful, that's all."

"Grateful?" The word was as sharp as a knife. "What exactly did you do to make him so grateful?"

"Nothing. He's had some problems, and I've been tutoring him, that's all."

"Tutoring? So, what, you're with him once a week?"

"Two or three times actually."

"So you're seeing this guy a couple of times a week, and he's so thrilled he's kissing you?"

"What about you and Danny?"

"That's different."

"Morgan saw you with her at the mall yesterday."

That seemed to knock him off balance.

"I had some errands to do. I ran into her. That's all."

"So it was an accident?" I knew how I sounded—bitchy and suspicious—but I didn't care.

"She's an old friend," Nick said. He sounded tired and angry. "And a good one."

"You mean it wasn't an accident you were with her at the mall?"

"Danny's family used to live in the apartment next to ours. Her room was right next to mine, and the walls were pretty thin. She heard a lot of the stuff that went on. You know what I mean, right?"

I had a pretty good idea. Nick's stepfather used to beat up on Nick's mother. On Nick too.

"We had this secret code. I'd be in my room, you know, after Duane was through with me, and Danny would tap on the wall. I'd sneak out onto the balcony and she would come out of her place, and we'd hang out there and pretend we were explorers or something. Danny was really big on explorers. She used to read all about them. It made her mad that they were all men. You wouldn't believe it to look at her now, but she used to be a real tomboy type."

He was right. I didn't believe it.

"Her family moved about a year before my mother died," Nick said. "It was awful. The worst time of my life. I didn't have anyone to talk to anymore. After that, whenever Duane came after me, I just wished he would kill me. If it hadn't been for Joey, he might have. When I bumped into Danny this summer, I couldn't believe it. We talked for a couple of hours. It was like we'd never been separated. We just kind of picked up where we left off."

"Mm hmm." I tried to keep the bitterness out of my voice.

"She means a lot to me, Robyn. She got me through some really hard times."

"I wish the two of you nothing but happiness," I said. I turned to go back upstairs.

"Wait," Nick said. He reached for me, but I pulled back out of his way.

"Morgan saw you two together at the mall. She saw everything."

He knew what I meant. I could see it in his eyes. But he tried to bluff me.

"What does that mean—everything?"

I told him almost word for word what Morgan had told me. I had gone over it again and again. The words were etched into my brain.

Nick just stood there.

"So it's true," I said, my stomach churning.

"That she kissed me? Yeah, it's true. But it's not what you think."

"Really?"

Suddenly I wanted to hurt him as much as he was hurting me.

"I went to James's house for dinner," I said. "I had a great time. He's a nice guy. We have a lot in common."

"What's that supposed to mean?"

"It means what it means," I said. "I wish you happiness with Danny. I hope you'll wish me happiness with James."

Nick's eyes burned into mine. "So now you're going out with him?"

"Like you said, you and Danny have a lot in common. So do James and I."

"Come on, Robyn. You acted like a total diva at that party, and you're acting like a diva now."

"I am not. I'm telling you how I feel. I'm wishing you well." Tears stung my eyes, but there was no way I was going to let him see me cry. "I have to go. I have to get ready for school."

I turned and ran back up the stairs.

Nick didn't try to stop me.

.   .   .

A few hours later I was at my locker, cramming my books into it and wishing I was somewhere else—wishing I was with Nick. Wishing it was some other time, too—maybe back in the summer on one of the weekends when he'd come up to Morgan's cottage. Or even before

119

then, maybe at the end of the school year, when Nick hadn't been as busy as he was now, when we'd taken long walks together, just the two of us—well, the two of us and Orion—and it had been enough for both of us to just hold hands. Back when we hardly even needed to talk.

Or maybe that was part of the problem. Maybe we hadn't talked enough. Maybe I'd just assumed that Nick was happy, that he was comfortable in the silence. He was different around Danny. Not so quiet. He talked to her. He had told her his dreams. A vet—it had never crossed my mind that that was what he wanted to be. Worse, I'd never thought to ask about his plans for the future.

"Are you okay?" said a voice behind me. Morgan. I looked over my shoulder at her. "What's wrong?" she said as soon as she saw the expression on my face.

"What isn't?"

"Nick?"

I nodded. He was problem number one.

"Did you talk to him?"

"This morning."

"And?"

"We had a fight."

"Did you ask him about what I saw?"

"Yeah. Right after he told me that he's spending the first day off he's had in ages with Danny." Okay, so maybe that wasn't the point of the day, but that was how it was going to turn out—Nick and Danny together. "He really likes her, Morgan. I think he likes her more than he likes me."

Morgan looped her arm through mine. "Remember what you told Billy when I started going out with Sean?" she said.

I sure did. Morgan had dumped Billy for another guy. Billy had been devastated. He had tried everything he could to win her back—without success. So I had told him the only thing I could think of that made any sense: Get over it. Move on.

"It was good advice," Morgan said.

"But he didn't take it," I pointed out. "And he was right not to."

"That's only because Sean turned out to be such a jerk. Look, the thing is, Robyn, you and Nick have had an up-and-down relationship ever since you met. You're so different from each other."

"You and Billy are different from each other, too."

"Yes, but I've known Billy practically my whole life. All I'm saying is, if it's not going to work out with Nick, it's not your fault. You didn't do anything wrong. You've stuck by him no matter what."

"He saw James kiss me," I said. Problem number two.

Morgan's eyes widened.

"You kissed James?"

"No. James kissed me."

Morgan broke into an enormous grin.

"Morgan, about James—"

"It's weird, isn't it?" Morgan said.

"What is?"

"How Billy and James seem to have so much in common. How they're both so gentle and shy and they both adore animals. And James is really nice, Robyn. It's obvious he likes you."

He liked me so much that he had told me his deepest secret—unlike Nick.

"Speak of the devil," Morgan said. She nodded down the hall. I turned and saw James and Billy coming toward us, Billy matching his long-legged stride to James's slower pace. James looked shyly at me, and I don't think I imagined the apprehension on his face. He had asked me not to tell anyone his secret, and so far I hadn't.

Billy slipped an arm around Morgan's waist, and she nestled contentedly against him. James looked at me and frowned.

"Is something wrong?" he said.

Morgan glanced at me. I could practically read her thoughts: *Not only is he cute, but he's also sensitive; he's picking up on your mood, Robyn.*

"Just the usual," I said. "School. Homework. Same old same old."

"I know what you mean," he said. "Except I'm lucky enough to have an excellent math tutor to make my days a little easier."

Morgan beamed so brightly that a passerby would have thought she was the one who'd been complimented.

"So, what do you have planned for the weekend, James?" she said oh-so-innocently. I could have strangled her.

"I was just telling Billy that I have to drive up north."

Terrific. It looked like everyone had plans—except me.

"Where are you going?" Morgan asked.

"A town called Harris."

Morgan perked up immediately, and I knew why. According to her, the photos that we had seen in James's cell phone had been taken in Harris. She glanced at me to see if I remembered.

"What's in Harris?" she said to James.

"My dad bought a place outside of town a few months ago. I have to go and clean it out."

"For the winter, you mean?"

"For good. We're selling it."

"So soon after you bought it? Is it built on a swamp or something?"

"My dad got a job offer." James turned to me. "A visiting professorship."

"Where?" I said.

"Australia. We're moving again." He sounded relieved—and no wonder. Australia was halfway around the world, far, far away from what had happened to his brother.

Morgan glanced at me. She looked stricken on my behalf.

"When are you leaving?" she said.

"He starts teaching in January, so we're leaving in December."

That was two months from now. In just two months, James would be gone. It was my turn to feel relieved. James didn't want me to tell anyone his secret. He didn't want anyone to know what had happened in that alley five years ago.

And as long as no one knew his secret, no one would ever know the crazy link between the two of us. He would never know.

James would never know that my mom was the lawyer who had grilled him on the witness stand that terrible day in court. He would never know that it was my mom who had made sure that the man who had shot his brother walked free. And if he never knew that, I would never have to face his hatred.

"You'll have an amazing time, James," I said. "You could take up surfing."

James looked down at his bad leg. "Well, I don't know about that." Then he flashed a smile. "But it will be different, that's for sure. I can't wait."

"James invited us all to go to Harris with him this weekend," Billy said.

"Well, actually, Billy offered to come," James said, the pink in his cheeks betraying his awkwardness.

"Four can get a lot more done than one, and in a lot less time," Billy said. "We can have that place cleaned out in no time. We can go up first thing Saturday morning—"

"I can't," Morgan said.

"Why not?" Billy asked.

There was a slight pause before she answered.

"Um, I have a hair appointment first thing Saturday morning."

I stared at her. She had had her hair cut and styled two weeks ago. *Liar!*

"Cancel it," Billy said. "You can get your hair done some other time."

Morgan looked aghast at the prospect.

"Not with Anthony, I can't. He's booked up a month in advance."

"So, wait a month," Billy said.

Morgan managed to look even more horrified.

Billy sighed. He turned to James.

"Well, I'll come," he said. "And so will Robyn."

What? I hadn't agreed to that.

"Well, I—" I stammered. I couldn't come up with an excuse as quickly as Morgan.

"I'll come too," Morgan said. "If you're willing to wait until late afternoon."

James frowned. "Well . . . My dad is having some packing stuff delivered in the morning. I have to be there to sign for it."

"Or," Morgan said, undeterred, "you and Robyn can go in the morning, and Billy and I will take the bus up later in the day. We can be there for dinner. Do you have a TV up there, James? We'll bring some movies. It'll be fun. Don't you think, Robyn? Unless you have something else planned?"

She knew perfectly well that I didn't. Half of me wanted to strangle her. The other half thought that she might have a point. Maybe helping James would get my mind off Nick.

"I'd be glad to help," I said to James. He smiled gratefully.

"Do you want me to bring my camera?" Morgan said. "You know, so we can take some pictures."

Could she be any less subtle?

"Why don't you?" James said. "I wouldn't mind a few pictures. You guys have been so great." He beamed at me.

"Do you have a camera, James?" Morgan said. "Do you know anything about photography?"

I could have kicked her.

"Absolutely nothing," he said.

Morgan looked significantly at me.

"Morgan has a really good camera," Billy said. "She can be the official photographer."

James looked at each of us in turn.

"You mean it?" he said. "You guys really want to help?"

"Sure," Billy said. "Why not?"

James turned shyly to me. "I can pick you up first thing Saturday morning."

"Perfect," Morgan said. "Billy and I will take the bus up after my appointment, and we can all drive back to-gether Sunday evening. What do you say, James?"

James didn't hesitate. "Okay." Then, in a quieter voice, he said to me, "At first I didn't think I would miss anything or anyone here. Now I'm not so sure."

Morgan was right. He was a sweet guy. Was it possible that a couple of months from now I might be sorry that he was leaving?

. . .

"Gregory Johnson?" my dad said that afternoon after school. He was dressed for work at the warehouse and was hunting through his desk for something. "You mean that kid who was shot a few years ago? What brings him to mind, Robbie?"

"We're doing a unit on law in my social studies class," I said. "My teacher mentioned it."

"She did?" My dad frowned. "I can't imagine why. As far as I can recall, the case didn't set any precedents."

"So you remember it?" I knew he would. My father might forget anniversaries and birthdays, but he never forgets anything related to criminal justice.

"Sure. In what context did it come up?"

"My teacher mentioned it in passing," I said. "She was talking about eyewitness evidence."

My dad nodded. "That was a big factor in the case, that's for sure." He paused. "You haven't talked to your mother about this, have you?"

"Why?"

"Well, it was her first murder case. And she took a lot of flak for it."

"She did?" I knew the case had been important to her. She had worked on it night and day. But I didn't know that she'd been criticized because of it.

"The eyewitness to the murder was the victim's brother. He was just a kid himself. Couldn't have been more than twelve or thirteen. And your mother—let's just say that not everyone appreciated how thoroughly she did her job."

"What do you mean?"

"Some people said that she was a little too aggressive in cross-examining the kid."

"Did you think that?"

My dad stopped his search and looked closely at me.

"What's this all about, Robbie? Did your teacher say something to you?"

"I'm just asking, Dad."

He sank down onto his desk chair.

"As I recall, the description the boy gave, combined with descriptions from a couple of people who had seen Eddy Leonard in the area before the murder, is what led the police to Leonard. The boy identified him out of a police lineup. He said he had no doubt who he had seen holding the gun in the alley that night, and that was the testimony he gave during the examination in chief. Then . . ."

He paused. "Did your teacher say something about your mom? Is that it? Because it has nothing to do with you. You don't have to feel like you have to defend—"

"It was nothing like that," I said. "It just came up in passing, and I remembered the name. I thought maybe I'd do my project on the case."

My dad looked surprised.

"Are you sure, Robbie? Because—"

"It would make a great project, Dad. And the fact that Mom was involved makes it even more interesting."

"I don't know if your mother would feel the same way."

"So what do you think, Dad? Do you think Mom was too aggressive?"

"Everyone is entitled to the best defense, Robbie."

"I know."

"And the burden of proof is on the prosecution. It's up to them to prove guilt beyond a reasonable doubt."

"I know that, too, Dad."

"It's the defense attorney's duty to mount a vigorous defense and to question the case made by the prosecution." He paused and studied me again. "That's what happened in the Leonard case."

"Then why did you and Mom argue so much about it at the time?"

"You remember that, huh?"

I nodded.

"Well, that was hardly our best year together."

"Even so, you wouldn't have argued if you thought Mom had done the right thing."

My dad shook his head. "I don't know where you're going with this," he said. "But I'm not going to do it, Robbie."

"Not going to do what?"

"Criticize your mom in front of you. She was just doing her job, and she did it well."

"You mean because she got Eddy Leonard off?"

"I mean because she's a good lawyer. She gave the jury reasonable doubt. And in a case like that, that relies almost exclusively on eyewitnesses, the judge's words to the jury worked to her advantage."

"What do you mean?"

"There have been a lot of studies on eyewitness IDing," my dad said. "They show that less than one-third of eyewitnesses make accurate identifications. Less than a third. Eyewitness mistakes are one of the main causes of wrongful convictions. It's such a big problem that there's even case law on the subject. In cases where the accused is ID'd by only one eyewitness, a judge has to warn the jury about the potential weakness of eyewitness identification—that well-intentioned eyewitnesses have made honest mistakes, and as a result, people have been wrongfully convicted."

"And the judge did that?"

My dad nodded.

"Do you think Eddy Leonard really did it, Dad? Do you think he killed Greg Johnson?"

He refused to answer.

"Okay," I said. "Can I ask you something else?

Was anyone else ever convicted of murdering Greg Johnson?"

"Not to my knowledge," my dad said. Given the keen interest with which he followed the crime beat, that meant no. Greg Johnson's murderer had gone unpunished. "Charlie Hart was involved in the investigation. If you really want to do a project on the case, you should talk to him."

"Do you think he'd mind?"

"I can call and ask him. I also know a reporter who covered the trial. I'll see what he can dig up for you. But I don't know how much you want to get into this with your mom. She got a pretty rough ride from some people, Robbie. It hurt her."

He went back to rooting around in the drawer for whatever it was he was looking for.

I said I'd keep quiet about it. "Oh, by the way, Dad, Morgan and Billy and I are going up north this weekend with James Derrick."

"James Derrick? Do I know him?"

I hesitated. I didn't want to lie to my dad, but I didn't want to get involved in a big discussion about James, either, especially after my promise to him.

"He's new at school this year," I said. "He and Billy have turned out to be good friends. And I've been tutoring him."

"Oh?" He arched an eyebrow.

"Just tutoring, Dad."

"Oh. Well, have a good time then." He pulled out an

envelope and inspected it. "Aha!"

"Have you talked to Mom lately, Dad?"

"No. Why?"

"Just wondering."

My dad stuffed the envelope into the pocket of his plaid work shirt. "I have to get to work, Robbie. See you later, okay?"

He called me that night to tell me that Charlie Hart would be happy to talk to me after school the next day.

CHAPTER **FOURTEEN**

C harlie Hart waved to me from a booth as soon as I stepped into the restaurant. He stood up when I approached him.

"Good to see you again, Robyn," he said, shaking my hand. "It's been a while."

The last time I had seen Charlie Hart, he had been investigating the murder of a hockey star (and Morgan's boyfriend at the time), Sean Sloane.

"You're keeping safe, I hope," he said, sliding back into the booth. A waitress appeared, order pad in hand. "Are you hungry, Robyn?" Charlie Hart said.

"No," I said. "But go ahead, please."

He ordered something to eat. "So, Mac said you wanted to talk to me about the Gregory Johnson shooting. He said it was for a school project."

I nodded. The trouble with lying is that it almost never stops with one lie. I had lied to my mom about why I'd asked about the Eddy Leonard case, because I'd promised James I wouldn't say anything to anyone about it. So then I had to lie to my dad too. And now here I was, lying to Charlie Hart.

"What subject?" Charlie Hart asked.

"Social studies."

"School sure has changed since I was there," he said. "I sure don't remember any discussion of murder trials. I might have paid more attention if there had been. How can I help you?"

"I'm trying to find out how the guy who killed Gregory Johnson got off."

The waitress returned with his order—steak, a baked potato, and some wilted green beans. Charlie waited until she had left again before he said, "Are you sure you don't want to talk to your mother about that? After all, she—"

"My dad said you'd be a good person to talk to. He said it was your case."

"I got the call, yeah."

"I heard there was an eyewitness."

"The brother," Charlie Hart said. "He was twelve when it happened, thirteen by the time the case went to trial. The officers on the scene said the kid was in shock when they got there. White as a ghost, trembling all over. Poor kid. I think about him every now and then— I wonder how he and his parents are doing. You lose a child like that family did, and it can tear the family apart. I've seen it happen."

"What I don't understand is, the brother—"

"David," Charlie Hart said. "The brother's name was David."

"He saw what happened. He was right there. He described the person who did it. And you arrested someone who matched that description, didn't you?"

"Yeah, the kid gave us a description—after he could talk."

"What do you mean?"

"Like I said, the kid was in shock. At first he didn't say a word. Just kept shaking and crying. Even his dad couldn't calm him down. But eventually he pulled himself together and told us what had happened—well, enough that we could make some sense of it. The kid was numb. Some things he remembered clear as a bell. Other things..." Charlie Hart shrugged. "It's tough enough when something like that happens. But when it's a kid?" He shook his head. "He gave us a description. And once he started, he didn't seem to be able to stop. He kept saying the same thing over and over. The description matched up with a guy my partner knew from before he transferred to Homicide—a small-time crook who lived in the neighborhood."

"Eddy Leonard."

Charlie Hart nodded. "We showed the kid a photo array. By then he'd clammed up again. He took it really hard. Well, who wouldn't, especially at that age? The kid was clinging to his dad's hand the whole time. But he picked out Leonard. Said he was the guy. We showed the pictures around, and a couple of other people picked out Leonard. They said they'd seen him in the vicinity before the shooting. Leonard had a record, so we picked him up. He didn't have an alibi. We asked him if he'd agree to be in a lineup, mostly to see how he'd react, if he'd ask for a lawyer, who would for sure object. Suspects have the right to refuse lineups. But Leonard said, sure, he'd do it. He didn't even want to consult a lawyer."

I stared at him. Even I knew enough to be surprised at that.

"Why would he agree to be in a lineup if he didn't have to—especially if he did it?"

Charlie Hart just shrugged. "You never know. Some of the guys we pick up—a depressingly large number of them—aren't too bright. A lot of them act against their own best interests. Don't ask me why. He agreed, and the kid identified him. Said he was positive Leonard was the guy who killed his little brother. He was unshakable. He kept going over the details." Charlie dug in his jacket pocket for a notebook and flipped it open. "I went back into my files," he said. "The boy described the shooter as having dark eyes, a long, thin nose, ears that stuck out a little, shaggy brown hair, small mouth, with a scar on his chin. Said it over and over, like he was afraid he was going to forget. The description matched Eddy Leonard. And the kid picked Leonard out—twice."

"So why wasn't Leonard convicted?"

"Well, for one thing," Charlie Hart said with a wry smile, "he had a good lawyer. And I guess, as a result of her cross-examination, the jury had its doubts. After all, we had absolutely no physical evidence to tie Leonard to the scene. Never found the gun. There were no fingerprints, no usable footwear impressions, no blood on any clothes of Leonard's that we found, no gunshot residue. Your mother also introduced Leonard's criminal record. Leonard had been arrested and convicted maybe half a dozen times, but he'd never used a gun—any weapon, for that matter. He'd never stolen a car. He was strictly burglaries, nothing violent, nothing confrontational. Your mother called a couple of cops who knew Leonard. She called some of his friends. They all made the same point. Put that together with the cross-examination of the brother, and your mom handed the jury reasonable doubt. The kid admitted that he'd been focused on his brother. The gun he described was a lot bigger than the gun that was used to shoot the little boy—but that's understandable. Most people come face-to-face with a bad guy and a loaded weapon, they focus on that weapon. And to a kid, it must have looked as big as a cannon."

That's what James had said.

"The kid also got all mixed up when he was asked how he knew Leonard was the guy. He said Leonard was wearing a blue plaid shirt when he saw him. That didn't match what we got from the two witnesses who had seen Leonard in the area. But it did match what Leonard was wearing during the lineup. Your mother argued that maybe the kid picked out Leonard in the lineup because he felt he had to pick someone, even though he was told that the person who did it wasn't necessarily in the lineup. We tell everyone that. We don't want people to guess." Charlie Hart shook his head. "The kid was terrified. We had to reassure him over and over that the people in the lineup wouldn't be able to see him. Even so, he was shaking all over. I felt sorry for him. I felt even sorrier for the way it turned out—I'm not criticizing your mom, Robyn. She was doing her job, and she did it well." He sounded exactly like my dad. "But in the end, all we had was a shaky eyewitness ID, which the judge had to caution the jury about—faulty eyewitness identification is one of the leading causes of wrongful convictions." So my dad had said. "And, like I said, we had no physical evidence, no corroborating witnesses, nothing like that."

"But you said two people had seen Leonard in the area."

"They did," Charlie Hart said. "But they saw him before the shooting. No one except that kid saw Leonard pull the trigger. No one else was anywhere near the car when it happened." He shook his head. "I felt sorry for him even before the trial. It's hard enough to see something like that happen. But with a dad like that . . ."

"What do you mean?"

"When I talked to him—the father—he said he'd heard shots. He said as soon as he realized what they were and where they had come from, all he could think about was his son."

"You mean, his sons."

Charlie Hart shook his head. "He said son." I frowned. "I know," he said. "It sounded strange to me too. But that's what he said. I found out later that the older boy is the *step*son." He sighed. "What can I say? Some guys are like that—it's the blood tie that matters to them. They can never truly accept another man's son as their own."

"But he stood by his stepson the whole time, didn't he?"

"Yeah, he did."

"Did you ask him about what he saw?"

"What do you mean?"

"On his way to the alley, he saw Leonard, too, didn't he? He saw someone hurrying away from the scene. He said he wished he'd taken a closer look." Which just proves how chaotic everything was. He'd heard something, but he'd been so focused on Greg that he hadn't taken a good look at the man who was running from where his son was.

Charlie Hart looked quizzically at me.

"I don't recall anything like that," he said. "Where did you hear it?"

I was pretty sure that's what James had told me. His father had seen a man hurrying away from the alley while everyone else was moving toward it. Surely James wasn't mistaken about that. Or was he? After all, he'd made a mistake about what Leonard was wearing that night.

"I thought that's what happened," I said.

"If it had, I would know," Charlie Hart said. "It was

my case. I don't remember the father saying he saw Leonard. Where are you getting your information?"

"I thought I heard it somewhere." I changed the subject. "Did Eddy Leonard have a family?" I was thinking about the threats that James told me Leonard had made.

Charlie Hart looked surprised at the question. "He had a wife and daughter. But, the way I heard it, the wife left him while he was in pre-trial custody. Took the little girl with her. Leonard took that hard. I don't know if he ever managed to track them down. The father told me that Leonard threatened his son, David, after the trial. Said Leonard blamed him for busting up his family. Apparently Leonard called the Johnson home a couple of times after that and made some more threats."

"Did the police do anything?"

"We had a talk with Leonard. We warned him that if he kept it up, he would be charged. He was really broken up. He said his missed his little girl. It was probably better for everyone when the Johnsons moved out of town." Charlie Hart eyed me speculatively. "I can't tell who you remind me of more, Robyn—your mother or your father. You ever thought of joining the force?"

. . .

Someone knocked on my father's door just as I was getting ready to go to school the next day.

"Get that, will you, Robbie?" my dad called from his office.

I got up off the couch where I was sorting through what I needed for the day and went to answer the door.

It was Nick. He looked uncomfortable.

"Is your dad here?"

I glanced back at my dad's office.

"He's on the phone," I said. "You want to wait for him?"

"No, it's okay," Nick said. "Can you just give him this for me?" He handed me an envelope.

"What is it?"

"It's for your dad," he said brusquely. Then he relented. "It's my notice."

"Notice?"

"That I'm moving."

My stomach did a lurch. "Moving?" I thought about Danny. Nick had said that her dad had built up a successful business, just like my dad had. I wondered if he owned a building too. "Where to?"

"I haven't figured that out yet."

He was moving, but he hadn't figured it out where he was going to live? Was he that desperate to get away from me?

"You need someplace to stay, Nick."

"Danny's parents are going to let me crash in their basement until I can make other arrangements. I put it in writing for your dad, you know, so it's official. He'll probably want to rent out the place to someone else."

I couldn't believe it. I couldn't believe that he was leaving. Or that he was going to be living in Danny's house.

"And Robyn?"

I looked up into his purple-blue eyes.

"Say you look out the window and you see a guy humming while he's walking down the street. He looks like he's on top of the world. How do you know whether he's happy because he's about to marry the woman of his dreams or relieved because he just killed his worst enemy?" He didn't wait for an answer. "You don't," he said, "unless you saw what happened before or what happened after. You don't even know for sure if he's really happy at all. Maybe he's just trying to convince everyone that he is. You can say he seemed happy, and sure, that would be right as far as it went. But what you saw was only a little piece of it—that doesn't tell you the whole story."

"Nick, I—"

"Tell your dad I'll be gone at the end of the month."

"But that's next week!"

"Yeah."

"Nick, about James—"

"I wish you happiness, Robyn. I do. You deserve a guy like James. He sounds nice. Reliable. And, like you said, you and he have a lot in common, just like Danny and me."

Danny again. My heart sank.

"I gotta go," he said.

I watched him walk down the stairs. He didn't turn back, not even once. After his footsteps had faded into nothingness, I closed the door and looked down at the envelope he had given me. This was it. After all the ups and downs we'd had over the past year, this was really it. Nick was leaving my life forever. I felt empty inside.

"Did I hear Nick?" my dad said. He was pulling on a jacket as he came out of his office, but he stopped when he saw my face. "Is everything okay, Robbie?"

"Yeah." I had to swallow hard to keep the quaver out of my voice and the tears out of my eyes. "Nick said to give you this."

I handed him the envelope. My dad barely glanced at it. "Is it important? Because I'm running late."

He began to study me closely.

"Are you sure you're okay, Robbie?"

"I'm fine."

"Problems with Nick?"

That did it. Tears trickled down my cheeks.

"He's moving out, Dad."

"Is that what this envelope is about?"

I nodded.

"I'm sorry, Robbie. What happened?"

"He met someone else—an old friend." More tears dribbled down my face. My dad put his arm around my shoulder.

"I wish I could stay, Robbie," he said. "But this job—"

"It's okay, Dad."

He kissed me on the forehead. "I won't be home until late. I have to be at the warehouse. We'll talk first thing tomorrow, I promise. I'll take you to breakfast, and you can tell me everything."

"I'm supposed to be going up north," I said. Now it was the last thing I wanted to do. "But I think I'll stay home."

"Maybe you should go, Robbie. Keep busy. Have some fun. Talk things over with Morgan. It might help."

Maybe he was right.

"Are you all going to Morgan's place?"

I shook my head.

"We're going to James's place. It's in Harris."

My dad smiled. "It's that time of year," he said. "Fall fair season." A dreamy expression came into his eyes. "Your mother and I used to drive up north every year to see the leaves change and visit the fall fairs. There's nothing like the woods in autumn, with all those leaves on the ground." I wondered how he would react to the possibility that my mother was moving clear across the country. He sighed. "Go with your friends. Have a good time. Let them cheer you up, Robbie. We'll talk when you get back."

"That won't be until late Sunday afternoon," I said.

"Perfect. We'll have dinner together downstairs. Make sure your phone is charged, and keep it on, okay?"

"Sure thing."

"By the way, how did it go with Charlie?"

"Okay, I guess."

"I talked to that reporter I told you about. He sent over a file of clippings on the case. It's on my desk, if you're interested."

"Thanks, Dad."

. . .

"You were right," I said to Morgan. We were in the girls' restroom at school. She passed me another tissue. I wiped my eyes and blew my nose. "Nick and Danny are more than just friends."

"Oh, Robyn, I'm so sorry," Morgan said.

I cried some more.

"It's good we're getting out of town for the weekend," Morgan said.

"That's what my dad said."

"Well, he's right. I'm not saying you're going to forget about Nick overnight, but maybe it'll help to spend some time with a guy who appreciates you. James likes you, Robyn. He really does."

Maybe. But he probably wouldn't if he knew who my mother was.

"I don't know, Morgan," I said. There was a big part of me that wanted to spend the weekend alone, feeling sorry for myself. "Maybe it would be better if . . ."

"We're going, and that's that," Morgan said just as the bell rang. "I have to run. Mr. Lowney gets really pissy when anyone is late for homeroom. I'll see you at lunch, okay?"

. . .

That night, after I finished packing for my trip to the country, I picked up the folder that my dad had left for me on his desk. It was filled with his reporter friend's coverage of the trial. There was even a picture of James—much younger—in one of the newspaper clippings. He was wide-eyed and looked frightened. I read through article after article. Most of what I read wasn't new. I'd heard it from James or my father or Charlie Hart. But it was still interesting. As I read I began to wonder, especially when the articles mentioned my mother. I knew my mom worked hard. She was a perfectionist, and not just at her chosen profession. How many times had I teased her about her obsessive sense of order and the long hours she put in at her desk in her home office? But I had never seen her in a courtroom. I began to imagine her, conservatively dressed in a dark business suit, probing, prodding, asking question after question, pointing out any inconsistencies in what witnesses said, poking holes in the prosecution's case, doing everything she could to provide her client with the best possible defense.

Because James was the only eyewitness, the reporter had devoted a lot of space to his testimony and cross-examination. First James was questioned by the prosecutor, who led him through what he had seen and heard in the alley the night his brother was shot.

The reporter noted that James—David—had gone into heart-wrenching detail about seeing his little brother lying bleeding on the ground in front of his eyes. He'd described the blood that completely soaked his brother's T-shirt and that pooled around his head and torso. He'd described his brother looking up at him and trying to say something. He'd described holding his brother's hand and how white it had been against all that blood, and then how still. James's parents, the reporter noted, had wept silently as they listened to his testimony.

Then the prosecutor had asked James about the man who had shot his brother. The description, noted the reporter, was more succinct, less detailed, rattled off: "The witness described the shooter as having dark eyes—he said he couldn't tell exactly what color they were—a long, thin nose, ears that stuck out, shaggy brown hair, a small mouth, and a scar on his chin." I stared at the words. They were almost identical to the words Charlie Hart had read to me out of his notebook—and to the description James had given me a full five years after the shooting. Charlie Hart had said that James had repeated the words over and over again, like he was afraid he was going to forget them. Well, he sure hadn't. They had burned themselves into his brain.

After the prosecutor had led James through everything he had seen and heard, my mother stood up to conduct her cross-examination. I trembled a little as I read what the reporter had written. I knew the story from James's point of view. He felt that he'd been attacked, that he'd been disbelieved, that the defense attorney—my mother—had treated him unfairly. He blamed himself for not standing up to her, for not insisting on what he had seen. But as I read the reporter's account, I began to see things a little differently.

My mom had started by asking James to describe the events leading up to the shooting. He responded by telling her about going to the movie and then heading back to the car with his brother while his dad stopped off at a convenience store.

And what about the actual shooting, my mom had asked. Could he describe what had happened in that alley?

"That man shot my brother," James had said. "The man had a gun and he shot Gregory."

"But how did it happen?" my mom asked. "What exactly did you see?"

"The man shot Gregory."

"Yes, but what did you see? What happened leading up to the shooting?"

James didn't answer the question other than to repeat what he had already said: "The man shot my brother."

Next, my mom asked, "Did you actually see the man shoot your brother?"

James had answered by saying, "That man shot my brother." He pointed at Eddy Leonard. "That man shot my brother. That man killed my brother." He burst into tears. He was so distraught that the judge called for the court to adjourn so that James could compose himself.

Shortly after court resumed, James slipped up. My mom asked more questions about what it had been like in the alley—how dark it was, whether there were any light sources, where exactly he had been.

"I was with my brother," James said. "I was with him the whole time."

That didn't sound right; James had told me that Greg ran into the alley ahead of him. He said that he'd gone into the alley after him.

My mom had asked James about the gun. Hadn't he told the police that it was "huge"? James agreed that he had. My mom produced the gun.

"Does it look big now, here in court?"

James had stared at it and admitted that it didn't. The reporter noted that James had sounded surprised.

"Can you describe how you were feeling in that alley, when you saw that gun?"

"I was afraid. That man shot my brother."

"Were you afraid he was going to shoot you?"

"I was afraid," James said again.

"What were you looking at?"

"I was looking at my brother. He was lying on the ground."

"Didn't you tell the police you were looking at the gun?"

James said that, yes, he'd been looking at that too.

Then my mom asked him, if he was afraid, if his brother was lying on the ground, and if he was focused on his brother and on the gun the man was holding, how he could describe the man so accurately? Was he sure that he'd had a really good look at him?

James had repeated the description that he'd given the police. Then, perhaps desperate to convince my mom, he added something new—something that he hadn't mentioned before. He'd said, "The man was wearing a blue plaid shirt."

According to the reporter, even the prosecutor had been taken aback by that.

My mom had asked James to clarify the matter: "He was wearing a blue plaid shirt?"

"The man who shot Gregory. He was wearing a blue plaid shirt," James had said.

"You saw the blue plaid shirt?" my mother had asked.

"Yes."

"Where did you see this blue plaid shirt?"

"When he shot my brother. The man who shot my brother was wearing a blue plaid shirt."

My mom had ended her cross-examination at that point.

The prosecutor spoke with James again after that, but James repeated his answer.

As the trial progressed, my mother questioned the two other people who had seen Eddy Leonard in the vicinity before the shooting. Both were sure about what he was wearing—a tan windbreaker over a white T-shirt. Neither had seen a blue plaid shirt. I remembered what Charlie Hart had told me: the only time that Eddy Leonard had been seen wearing a blue plaid shirt was during the lineup. I wondered if it were possible that Charlie Hart was right. Had James picked Leonard out of the lineup simply because he believed that the guilty man was in the lineup somewhere? Or had it happened the way James had told me—had he made a mistake because he'd been so flustered by my mom's questions? If that were true, why had he repeated his mistake when the prosecutor had asked about the blue shirt?

After the prosecution had finished its examination, my mom called her witnesses. One of the articles included an artist's sketch of Leonard—a skinny, clean-shaven man in a dark suit. When Leonard took the witness stand, my mom had even asked him about his criminal record. Leonard had replied "in a straightforward fashion," according to the reporter. He had been convicted several times of petty theft and breaking and entering. He had never used a weapon and had never been found in possession of a weapon.

Later my mom called other witnesses, including two police officers, who backed this up. She asked Eddy Leonard if he knew that there was no law that could compel someone accused of a crime to participate in a police lineup. He said that a lawyer had told him that once. Then why, my mom had asked, had he agreed to participate in this particular lineup? His answer: because he hadn't done anything wrong.

The last article in the series—after Eddy Leonard had been acquitted of the murder charge—focused on my mother's handling of the case. Richard Johnson— James's father, Mr. Derrick—was quoted extensively. He said he was "outraged" at his son's treatment by the defense and stunned by "the sleazy tactics." I was surprised to see him described as a professor of law and the author of more than ten books on the development of law and legal systems. I remembered what he had said at dinner that night—that he had written a book on the history of everyday things. He'd said the topic was a departure for him, but still, I had assumed that he was a history professor. It had never crossed my mind that his area of expertise was law.

Public opinion seemed to side with James's dad and against my mom. Several people were quoted as saying that a guilty man had gone free and that it was the defense's fault. One woman said she thought it was "shameful how that young boy was treated and made out to be a liar." The article attempted to be balanced by pointing out the weaknesses with eyewitness identification. It also highlighted the lack of any physical evidence that could have corroborated the eyewitness testimony at the trial.

I closed the file folder and sat there, thinking. I could understand why James felt that he'd let his brother down, why he blamed my mother. But now that I had read about the trial, I wasn't so sure I agreed. My mom had just done her job. She'd done it well. And for that she had drawn a lot of criticism. I was sorry about how James felt. I was even sorrier that his brother's killer had never been brought to justice. I couldn't imagine how it must feel to know that that man was out there somewhere, secure in the knowledge that he had gotten away with murder.

The phone rang. I jumped. I hoped it was Nick.

CHAPTER **FIFTEEN**

I scrambled for the phone. It was Charlie Hart.

"I don't know how you knew, Robyn, but it turns out you were right," he said. "I tracked down the first officer on the scene the night Greg Johnson was shot. It was in his notes—Richard Johnson told him that he'd seen someone suspicious. He said the guy was hurrying away from the scene and that he got a good look at him."

"Was it Eddy Leonard?"

"Well, that's the thing," Charlie Hart said. "He gave a description. Then he changed what he'd said. He told the officer that everything had happened so fast, it was all a big blur. He said he couldn't remember who or what he'd seen. He'd heard a bang, then a scream—that was the older boy. After that, he saw faces but they all kind of blended together. There were a lot of people on the street, and one of them struck him as odd because he was moving away from the sound of the shot, whereas other people were looking in the direction of the noise. But he said he wasn't sure who was who—there were too many people, and he didn't want to mislead anyone or send them in the wrong direction. Apparently he was distraught, very apologetic. The officer he spoke to should have briefed me or my partner on that, but he was new, inexperienced. Instead, he told us what he thought were the facts—that Richard Johnson had heard the shots and the scream, but he hadn't seen anything. And when I spoke to Richard Johnson—which I did on numerous occasions—that's what he told me."

James hadn't mentioned anything about his father making a statement to the police and then withdrawing it. But he'd been in shock. Maybe he'd forgotten. Or maybe his father hadn't told him.

"Thing is," Charlie Hart continued, "the officer called me back a couple of hours after I spoke to him. He'd dug out the notebook he used at the time and taken a look at what Johnson had told him. And you know what? That first description he gave to the officer—it matched what the boy told us."

"What do you mean?"

"I mean it really matched—dark eyes, long, thin nose, ears that stuck out, shaggy brown hair, scar on his chin. He was definitely describing the same person that the boy said he'd seen. If we'd known that . . ." His voice trailed off.

"If you'd known, what would you have done?" I said.

"Well, for one thing, Richard Johnson could have been called to testify. It might have made a difference."

"Might have?"

"Well, it wouldn't have put Leonard at the scene of the shooting, and it wouldn't have put the gun in his hand. The boy was the only one who could do that. And we still didn't have any physical evidence. But it would have put Leonard close to the scene at the time of the shooting. On the other hand, the prosecution led with the boy, and your mom managed to plant a huge seed of doubt. And the other witnesses who saw Leonard only saw him before the shooting. They had no idea what he was doing in the area. He could have been on his way to an appointment or to meet a friend. They didn't even see him near that alley. So their evidence was pretty weak. After your mom managed to shake the boy, she had an easy time making her case. Without any physical evidence, the outcome probably would have been the same. Leonard would have walked."

He sighed. "In any event, the worst part of my job is having to deal with the victim's loved ones. We focused on the brother. He was young, he'd been right there, it was obvious he was in shock. Maybe we should have paid more attention to the dad. Maybe we underestimated how hard it had hit him."

"But you told me that he was with James the whole time—when he was looking at pictures and at the line-up. Wouldn't he have recognized Leonard when he saw him?"

"I like to think that if it had been me, I would have recognized him," Charlie Hart said. "But it happened right downtown, Robyn. There were a lot of people around. People can get really mixed up when they're under a lot of stress—and I can't think of anything more stressful than the murder of a child. I feel sorry for the brother, though. That kid had a lot riding on him."

He sure did. The whole murder case.

"I guess, if nothing else, it'll make an interesting sidebar for your project," Charlie Hart said. "It sure speaks to some of the problems with eyewitness IDing. You see a face in a crowd for a second or two. How well can the average person pick that person out again an hour later—never mind a day or a week or a month?"

"You said if you'd known, Johnson could have testified. Is there anything else you would have done if you'd known?"

For a moment he said nothing. Then, finally: "When I said the father's description matched the son's, I meant it, Robyn. They matched almost word for word. That doesn't happen very often. It makes a person wonder. It sure would have made me wonder."

. . .

My father had just appeared from his bedroom—his hair was disheveled, and he was wearing pajama bottoms and a T-shirt—when I spotted James's car pulling up at the curb below. Suddenly I was glad to be going. I was even more curious now about James and what had happened to him.

"I have to go, Dad," I said to my bleary-eyed father. "My ride is here. See you tomorrow."

My dad grunted at me as he made his way to the kitchen to put the coffee on.

I grabbed my things and ran downstairs.

James got out of the car to greet me. I threw my backpack and purse into the backseat. I was getting into the car when I heard a loud rowf. Nick and Orion were in the park across the street. Nick stared at me. Well, let him. He obviously didn't care about me. I met his eyes for a moment before getting into the front seat next to James.

. . .

We chitchatted until we were out of the city, and then James put some music on. We had been driving for nearly an hour when I glanced at him.

"It's great out here, isn't it?" he said, smiling at the fields on either side of the road.

"I always forget there's an 'out here' out here," I said. I told him about my summer in the country, but without mentioning Nick.

"Do you mind if we take a little detour?" he said when I'd finished.

"I thought you had to be up there in time to sign for something."

He grinned. "Change of plans. This weekend I tidy up the place. Next weekend, when my dad's around, we start to pack."

"Well then, let's take a detour."

He turned off the main road and followed a winding gravel road to a waterfall.

"We rented a place up here one summer when I was a kid. I loved to go behind the falls," he said. "I'd pretend I was an explorer. Or that I was sneaking up on the enemy."

"It's beautiful," I said.

We got out and walked around, and then, because I could see he was dying to, we picked our way across some rocks and slipped behind the cascading water. James smiled. He looked more content than I had ever seen him. He was still smiling when we started back down the gravel road to the highway.

This was my chance. I hesitated. I didn't want to ruin his mood. But I did want to know more about Eddy Leonard.

"Can I ask you something, James?" I said at last.

"Sure."

"I've been doing some reading about . . ." Why was it so hard to come out with it, to call it what it was? "About what happened to your brother."

I felt James tense up beside me. "Oh?"

"You said your dad told you that he'd seen someone hurrying away from the sound of the gunshots. He thought that was strange, right?"

"Yeah. Why?"

"Well, he said the same thing to the first police officer who arrived on the scene. He even described the man. But then he changed his mind and told the officer that he'd been wrong. He said that there were so many people on the street that when he heard those shots, all he could think about was his son."

James winced at the word. He glanced at me. "Where did you hear that?"

"I read it," I said, lying—again. It seemed kinder than telling him I had spoken to a detective. Or maybe I was just being a coward. "I'm sorry. After you told me, I went online."

He was silent for a moment. Finally, he said, "And?"

"Did your dad describe that man to you—the one he saw hurrying away from the alley?"

James's jaw tightened.

My dad is pretty good at reading people—at least according to Vern Deloitte, his business partner. My mom disagrees. In fact, I once even heard her ask Vern, "If Mac is so good at knowing what people think, why does he always act so surprised when I get mad at him for doing the same thing for the millionth time?" It was a good question.

I was good at reading some people. I could always tell when Nick was angry but was trying not to show it. I could tell when Morgan was irritated and was trying to hide it. Okay, maybe that was a no-brainer—Morgan never tried very hard. I would have bet my life that I had just struck a nerve with James. The thing I couldn't figure out was, which nerve?

"No, he didn't describe him."

"Are you sure? He didn't describe the man to you and ask you if he was the one who'd shot your brother?"

"No!" His hands were clenched on the steering wheel. His eyes were fixed firmly ahead, as if I were the last person on Earth he wanted to look at.

"I'm sorry," I said. "I just—" Just what? Don't understand? What was there for me to understand? Gregory Johnson was dead. Edward Leonard had walked on the charge. And James hadn't gotten over it. Maybe he never would, and who could blame him? And what was I doing? I was thinking about the mistakes that everyone had made—James, his father, the prosecutor, the police—everybody except my mom. She hadn't made any mistakes. It was everyone else who had messed up.

James had made a mistake when he'd insisted at the trial that he had seen something the night of the shooting he couldn't possibly have seen. Eddy Leonard hadn't been wearing a blue plaid shirt. Other witnesses corroborated that fact. Besides that, there were gaps in James's story. He hadn't answered all of my mom's questions. He hadn't told her how the shooting had actually happened. Why was that? Why hadn't he answered?

Then there was James's father. He had told the first officer on the scene that he'd seen someone hurrying away from where he'd heard the shots. Then he had changed his story. And, according to James, he had never described this man to James, had never asked James if the man he'd seen was the same one James had seen. Why not? And why hadn't he recognized Eddy Leonard in the photo array or at the lineup? He'd been right there with James, holding his hand. If he had recognized him, would he have strengthened the prosecution's case? Charlie Hart didn't seem to think it would have made much difference, given the lack of physical evidence. And, knowing what I knew, I had to agree with him. It probably didn't matter.

Then there was the prosecutor. Maybe if he had prepared James more carefully, James wouldn't have become so rattled on the stand. Maybe James wouldn't have confused what he saw at the lineup with what he had seen the night of the shooting—assuming that James had been confused and not mistaken.

The first officer on the scene, the one who had spoken to James's dad before the detectives arrived, had definitely messed up when he hadn't passed along everything that James's father had said. Maybe Charlie Hart had messed up too. Maybe if he had gone over everything carefully with the other officer when he arrived on the scene himself, he would have known what James's dad had seen. Maybe that would have changed something. Or maybe not. Sure, maybe Mr. Derrick had seen Leonard fleeing the scene. But that didn't put Leonard at the scene. It didn't put the gun in his hand—the gun that had never been found. It didn't have him pulling the trigger. James was the only one who could testify to those facts. James was the only real eyewitness.

James, who had insisted at the trial that he'd seen something he couldn't possibly have seen.

James, who had been rattled.

James, who had already been carrying a heavy burden. His little brother had almost died once before in James's care. And then, that night in the alley, James had been responsible for Greg—for Richard's son—and Greg had died. That was certainly bad enough. But then to stumble so badly during the trial, to feel responsible for letting the killer walk, to believe that the man he called Dad blamed him for that . . .

"I'm sorry, James," I said again. "I was just wondering, that's all."

James was silent for a few moments. A new song started to play.

Finally James said, "I told the cops. I told the prosecutor. I told everyone. He had dark eyes. He had a long, thin nose. He had ears that stuck out. He had shaggy brown hair. He had a small mouth. He had a scar on his chin, right here." He touched his own chin.

Those were the same words James had used when describing the man to Charlie Hart and that Charlie Hart had read to me out of his notebook. They were the same words he had used when he first described the man to me.

They were the same words he had used in court.

Always the same words.

Charlie Hart had said that after James had described the man he'd seen—and that had taken a while because

James had been so rattled that he'd been mute for an hour or more—he had repeated the description over and over. Charlie had said it was as if he didn't want to forget it. Or couldn't shake it. I could see that. But to still be using the same words, the same order, every time, after all these years? The only things I could do that with were song lyrics and a couple poems I'd been forced to learn by my seventh-grade teacher, who had insisted that everyone should know a few solid poems by heart.

"James, why did Eddy Leonard shoot Greg?" I said.

James tensed up again. "What do you mean?"

"I mean, what did Greg do?"

"He surprised him. We surprised him. The man was standing beside my dad's car when we went into the alley. He fired at Greg."

"You must have been afraid he was going to shoot you, too," I said. I sounded just like my mother had at the trial.

James didn't look at me.

"He shot Greg," he said. "Then he ran away."

"But weren't you afraid he was—"

"I don't want to talk about it, Robyn," James said. His face was white. "I'm sorry I ever brought it up."

I mumbled an apology and promised myself that I wouldn't mention it again. It had been a mistake to bring it up in the first place. The past was the past. But it kept eating at me. At first I'd thought my mom had been at fault. She had made it look like he wasn't sure what had actually happened.

But the more I found out, the more I began to wonder. James had described the aftermath of the shooting to me in detail, just as he had at the trial, but in different words, emphasizing different things. He had told me what he'd thought, what he'd felt, what he'd seen. But he had never told me—or anyone else, according to everything I had read or heard—about the shooting itself. Why had Eddy Leonard shot a nine-year-old boy? Was it because he was trying to steal James's father's car and he was afraid that the boys would identify him to the police? It seemed like an extreme response. And both boys had seen him. Both could have ID'd him. Why did he only shoot one of them? Especially since James could identify him as the man who had shot Greg?

And why had James's dad told the first cop on the scene that he had seen someone suspicious and could even describe him—using words almost identical to the description James would give—and then almost immediately change his story? What had made him decide he was wrong?

And why was it all bothering me so much? Why couldn't I let it alone?

"It's just that I know you feel terrible that your dad blames you for what happened," I said softly. "But it could have happened to you too, James. The man shot your brother. It's a miracle he didn't shoot you. I mean, you were right there. You saw him."

"I said, I don't want to talk about it," James said, his voice so sharp that I jumped.

Let it alone, I told myself. *Leave him alone. You're just stirring up bad memories.* I even had a pretty good idea now why he was so angry. It was because he hadn't been shot. Because he thought that his dad probably wished it had been James shot dead and Gregory still alive. Because he had let his brother and his parents down when he'd fallen apart on the witness stand. Because he felt responsible for the killer walking free.

"It happened," he said, trying to control himself. "Greg got killed. I should have been"—he broke off and drew in a deep breath. "The guy shot Greg. I saw him. He had dark eyes. He had a long, thin nose. He had ears that stuck out. He had shaggy brown hair. He had a small mouth. He had a scar on his chin. He killed my little brother, Robyn. Greg was lying on the ground. He looked so small. And he was looking up at me. Like he was wondering how I could have let something like that happen to him . . . I want to forget it. I just want to forget the whole thing. But I can't. It's like a nightmare. Or like a movie that keeps playing and playing and that I can't turn off."

"I'm sorry," I murmured again.

James was silent for a moment. Then he said, "I want to have some fun for a change. You can't believe how much I've been looking forward to this weekend. It's a chance to get away. We can take a walk in the woods when we get there. Then we can drive into town and pick up Morgan and Billy. We can get something to eat, too. And there's this island in the middle of the lake. It's so peaceful. You'll love it."

I laughed. "I thought the whole point of the trip was to clean the place up so your dad can sell it. When were you planning to do that?"

"I'll get to it," James said, smiling. "I can always finish it next weekend."

I let him keep talking about the island and his plans for the day. He began to relax. I asked him how he felt about moving again so soon.

"It's on the other side of the world," he said. "Maybe if I get that far away, I can forget about everything."

Maybe. But I doubted it. You could never really escape your memories, especially bad ones like he'd been carrying around.

"I can't wait to go," he said. "I wish we could leave right now, after this weekend. I wish we could just move on before"—he broke off again.

"Before what?"

"I wish we could just leave. It was a mistake to come back here. I thought changing my name would make a difference, but it didn't. I thought if I went to visit Greg and told him how sorry I was, that would make a difference. I was wrong about that too. I thought . . . I thought a lot of things. But I see now that we were wrong. We never should have come back. I never should have let my dad talk me into it."

"James, I'm sorry," I said. "I didn't mean to ruin your weekend. It's just that I know you feel responsible for what happened, and when your dad told me about the car crash—"

James's head snapped around to look at me.

"He talked to you about that? What did he say?"

We turned off the highway and onto a gravel road into which countless vehicles had worn two deep parallel grooves.

"He just mentioned it," I said. "While we were waiting for you to come home for dinner that night."

James slowed the car down. The road was old and washed out in places. The trees were dense on either side, and there were no signs of life, let alone of other houses, along the desolate road.

"Hey, do you think we could take a picnic out to that island?" I said to lighten the mood. "What are the sunsets like up here?"

James brought the car to a stop and shut it off.

"What did he say about it, Robyn?"

"Nothing. Really. I don't even know why I brought it up. We came here to get some work done and have some fun. Coming back has been hard enough on you—"

"What did he tell you?" His eyes burned with emotion. His voice was quiet but insistent. "Please, I'm not mad at you. I won't get mad. It's just that after it happened, my dad and I never really talked about it. But he said something to you. What was it?"

I hesitated.

"Please, Robyn."

"He didn't say a lot, James. Seriously. Just that it happened two years after your mom died. And that the police thought it was an accident . . . He said he was in the car with you when it happened and he doesn't blame you for what happened."

"What?"

"He said you took your mom's death hard, which is totally understandable, and—"

"He doesn't blame me?" James said. "What's that supposed to mean?"

"He said you weren't yourself after your mom died. Grief affects different people in different ways."

"He doesn't blame me," James said again. He sat very still. With the car engine off, so far from the highway and from any houses or cabins, all I could hear were birds—calling, singing, telling each other their bird secrets.

"Is everything okay, James?"

He nodded—curtly, almost imperceptibly—but didn't look at me. He turned the key in the ignition and started the engine again. We drove farther down the sloping road, deeper into the woods, even farther from the main road.

Finally we turned onto an even narrower road—a driveway, it turned out. Moments later, a two-story, chalet-style house appeared, all rich brown wood and glinting windows against a slash of blue—a lake—behind it.

A red Honda sat on a patch of scrubby grass to one side of the driveway.

James frowned. "That's my dad's car," he said.

"When you said he went out of town, you didn't say this was where he went."

"I didn't know." He parked behind the other car.

We got out, and I started to open the back door to retrieve my purse and backpack.

"We can unload later," James said. "Let's see what's going on."

He approached the house cautiously. He did not seem pleased that his dad had shown up. It was becoming clearer and clearer to me that there was a lot of unresolved tension between father and son.

James climbed up onto the screened porch and opened the outer door.

"Hello?" he called.

"Is that you, Dee?" came Mr. Derrick's rich, deep voice. "Is Robyn with you?"

I joined James on the porch.

"Hello!" I called.

"Where are you, Dad?"

"In the kitchen. Come on through. And lock the front door behind you, will you, Dee?"

James's frown deepened, but he did as he was told. We walked through a large, sunny living room to the spacious kitchen at the back of the house. The kitchen overlooked another screened porch, through which I could see the dazzling blue of a vast lake dotted with treed islets. The view would have been breathtaking if I had been able to give it my full attention. But I was distracted—by the man kneeling on the kitchen floor with his hands clasped behind his head, and by the gun in Richard Derrick's gloved hand.

CHAPTER SIXTEEN

James stared first at the man on his knees and then at his father. My attention was riveted to the man. I recognized him even though I had never met him. It was the same man who had been in all those pictures on James's cell phone.

"What are you doing here?" James said to his father. "What's he doing here?"

Mr. Derrick shook his head slowly.

"We talked about this, Dee," he said. "We talked about it dozens of times."

My eyes went back to the gun. What was going on?

"You know the plan," Derrick said.

"Dad!" James looked frantically at me.

"It's all right," Mr. Derrick said. "We don't have anything to hide from Robyn. We talked about this, Dee. We talked about how it would go. He spotted us up here. He recognized us. He recognized you. He threatened to get

170

even with you back then. The police know he did. They have a record of it. And he's never forgotten that threat. He's never stopped blaming you for his family leaving."

The kneeling man looked up, and James met his eyes. The color drained from James's face. One of the man's hands reached out, groping for anything that could steady him. He found nothing.

"But I thought—"

"You thought what?" Mr. Derrick said.

"You got that new job in Australia. You're going back to teaching. I'm going to college. We're getting out of here. I thought we could put this behind us."

"Put it behind us?" Derrick said. He shook his head. "We came back here to take care of things, Dee. We talked about how this would happen. He saw you up here. He was determined to get even with you, and there was nothing we could do. He wanted payback for what he thinks you did to his family, in his pathetic mind. As if a murderer like him even deserves a family."

I stared at the kneeling man. Was it possible?

James looked at me again before turning back to his father.

"But, Dad, Robyn—"

"Ah," Mr. Derrick said. "Robyn." His eyes flicked to me. "Robyn, would you be so kind as to kneel down beside Mr. Leonard?"

I was right. The man on his knees was Eddy Leonard—the man who had shot James's brother and gotten away with it. He'd put on weight. A beard covered

171

the scar on his chin. But he still had a long, straight nose, dark eyes, and ears that stuck out from his head.

"Dad, what are you doing?" James said, horrified.

Derrick turned his icy hard eyes on me.

"Kneel," he ordered. "Now."

I stared at the gun in his hand. What would happen if I refused?

"Let me make myself clear," Mr. Derrick said when I hesitated. "This gun is loaded. When I tell you to kneel, please believe that there will be consequences if you don't."

"Dad, please," James said. "This has nothing to do with her."

"Kneel," Mr. Derrick said. The chill in his voice made my knees buckle. I sank to the floor.

"Dad, please!"

"Do you know who she is, Dee? Did she tell you?"

"What do you mean?" James said. "What are you talking about?"

Mr. Derrick repeated his question, emphasizing each word: "Do you know who she is?"

I had been dreading this moment, but never in my worst nightmares had I imagined how awful it would be.

I looked up at James. "I should have told you," I said. "I should have told you as soon as I realized."

"Realized what?" James said. "Told me what?"

"Her mother is that piece of scum's lawyer," Derrick said, jerking his head at Eddy Leonard.

Eddy Leonard looked at me for the first time. James stared at me too, his mouth agape. I should have told him. He might have hated me for it, but at least I would have been able to say that I'd done the right thing. As it was, I felt like a coward. James had bared his soul to me, and I had hidden something from him.

James shook his head, as if he couldn't believe what his dad was telling him. As if he refused to believe.

"But her name—" he said.

"She has her father's name. But her mother is Patricia Stone."

James was still shaking his head. "How long have you known? Why didn't you tell me?"

"It's part of the plan," Mr. Derrick said. "It's why we came back here. Now we can show that woman, Dee. We can show her what it feels like. That piece of garbage took Gregory away from me, and her mother let him get away with it. Now he's going to take her daughter away from her, and she'll have only herself to blame. If he'd been convicted four years ago, he would be behind bars now. But she kept him out, so now she has to pay. And so does he."

James stared at me. He looked betrayed and angry. And lost.

"Remember how we planned it, Dee," Derrick said, his voice soft and lilting as he tried to soothe James. "He broke in here, desperate to get even with you, just like everyone heard him say he would, just like he said he would do in those calls he made after the trial."

"I was drunk," Eddy Leonard said. "I was mad. But I never would have—"

"Shut up," Derrick said.

Leonard bowed his head.

Mr. Derrick turned back to James. "You and Robyn arrived to find him here, holding me at knifepoint. Remember how we said it would go, Dee?"

"You never said anything about her daughter," James said. "You never even told me she had a daughter."

"That lawyer has to pay, James. Listen to me. You had no choice. He had me at knifepoint, and he was waiting for you to arrive. He was going to kill us both, Dee. He said he was going to get even for his wife and child leaving him. But you fought back. You got away from him and got your grandfather's old gun out. You were just trying to make him put down the knife. It all happened so fast. You were terrified. You shot—but he had grabbed the girl for a shield. It happened so fast, Dee. You told him to put the knife down, but he didn't. You panicked and shot at him. It wasn't your fault that he grabbed the girl at the last minute. You shot her, but it wasn't your fault."

I was trembling all over. This couldn't be happening. It just couldn't.

"Then he came after you, Dee. You didn't have any choice. You shot again. It was self-defense. You don't have to worry, Dee. I saw it all. I'll tell them . . . No one will make a fool out of me. We're going to make them pay. We're going to make them feel what we felt."

"The police will investigate," I said. "They'll think it's a pretty big coincidence that Leonard and I happened to be here at the same time."

"James can honestly say he had no idea who you were. You said so yourself—you never told him. You never told me, either."

"My dad will never believe you. He used to be a cop. He'll get to the truth."

"I'm willing to take that risk," Mr. Derrick said. His voice was eerily calm. "So is Dee, aren't you?" he looked at James. "He promised me he'd make this right no matter what. Isn't that right, Dee? This man"—he glanced at Leonard—"murdered my son. And her mother saw that he got away with it. You're going to make it right, aren't you, Dee?"

I looked at James.

"You could go to prison," I said. "You could throw away your whole life."

Without taking his eyes off Eddy Leonard or me, Derrick handed James the gun. James looked down at the deadly object in his hand.

"You got it wrong, kid. You had it wrong all along," Eddy Leonard said. "I didn't kill your brother. I was never in that alley."

"Raise the gun, Dee," Derrick said. "You can do it. We talked about it, remember? You can do it." He turned to me. "Stand up."

"Look," Leonard said. "A person sees something like what you saw, in a dark alley like that, he don't always remember it right. Maybe the guy you saw was my height. Maybe he even looked like me. But it wasn't me. I wasn't—"

"Shut up," Mr. Derrick said. "It was you. I saw you with my own eyes. I saw you scuttling away from that alley like some kind of insect."

"I heard the shots, and I got out of the area fast, you bet," Eddy Leonard said. "I was trying to break into a shop a few doors up. I didn't want the cops to see me anywhere near there. But I wasn't in that alley. I didn't shoot that kid."

I stared at Mr. Derrick. So he had seen Eddy Leonard. The description he had given the first officer on the scene had been true, even though he'd later said he was mistaken.

The first officer on the scene had said that James was mute. In shock. It was only after Charlie Hart and his partner from Homicide had turned up that James had started talking, and then he had recited the description of the shooter over and over.

An idea took shape in my head.

Mr. Derrick had seen Eddy Leonard hurrying away from the alley.

Mr. Derrick would have known that any statement he made would be circumstantial—that just because Leonard had been near the alley, that didn't mean he had been in it, or that he had shot anyone. He would have known that James's statement was crucial if Leonard was to be convicted of murder—James was the only eyewitness. But he was also a badly shaken-up eyewitness who was mute from shock.

Mr. Derrick also would have known that when a crime was committed, the police kept witnesses separated. They didn't let them talk to each other because they were afraid that what one witness said would influence the other.

But the police had let Mr. Derrick stay with James every step of the way. Why? Because they didn't consider Derrick to be a witness. He had told the police that he hadn't seen anything.

James had already let his dad down once before. Greg had almost drowned, and Derrick had held James responsible. Then came the shooting in the alley. Greg was dead, and James was the only person who was able to make sure that justice was done.

James, who, when he had finally started to talk that night, had given Charlie Hart and his partner the exact same description of the shooter that his father had given to the first officer. He had repeated it over and over again so that he wouldn't forget it, just like he had repeated shopping lists and the errands he was supposed to do.

So that he wouldn't forget one of the most traumatic experiences of his life? An experience that had given him nightmares ever since? What would have made James think that he would forget something like that?

. . .

"Stand up," Mr. Derrick said again.

But I stayed on my knees and did my best to pretend that James wasn't pointing a gun at me.

"Look at him, James," I said. "Look at Leonard. He says he didn't do it. He says he was never in that alley. Look at him and tell me—is he the man who shot Greg? Not the man you saw in the lineup, or in court. The man you saw in the alley—is it him, James? Did you see him shoot your brother?"

James stared at Eddy Leonard. Just for a second, the gun trembled in his hand.

"James, is he the man you saw in the alley?" I said again. "Is he the one who shot Greg?"

"Don't listen to her, Dee," Mr. Derrick said. "Focus on the plan."

I forced myself to ignore Derrick. "What was he wearing, James?"

James looked blankly at me.

"You described him to me a couple of times, James, so you must remember. What was he wearing that night in the alley? You said you saw the gun. You said you saw his face. What was he wearing?"

James was trembling all over.

"Focus, Dee," Mr. Derrick said. "Focus."

"What was he wearing, James?"

That's when James did what I was afraid he would do: he turned to his dad.

"It's him, right, Dad?" he said. "He's the one, right?"

"Of course it's him," Mr. Derrick said. "I saw him

running away from the alley."

"What about you, James?" I said. "What did you see?"

"I just told you what he saw," Mr. Derrick said.

"You told me what you saw," I said. I looked at James. "What did you see, James?"

The hand holding the gun wavered again and then lowered.

"I don't know," he said softly.

Mr. Derrick grabbed my arm and, leaning heavily on his cane, tried to yank me to my feet.

"James, you said in court that the man you saw was wearing a blue plaid shirt," I said. "But Eddy Leonard wasn't. The night Gregory was shot, other people saw him. He was wearing a tan windbreaker."

James's shoulders slumped. He knew that already. I bet his dad had never let him forget it.

"You told me all about Greg," I said. "You told me how he looked up at you. You told me that he looked surprised. But you didn't tell me how it happened. You didn't tell me why he got shot. How did it happen, James? Why did Greg get shot?"

The hand holding the gun dangled uselessly at James's side.

"I don't know," he said.

Mr. Derrick held out his hand. "Give me the gun, Dee," he said.

I stood up slowly. Derrick yanked the gun out of his son's hand.

"Greg was fooling around," James said. He didn't seem to notice that his father had taken the gun away from him. "He was always fooling around. I had to grab him by the hand to get him to go with me to the car, like Dad said." He looked at his dad. "You said to wait for you at the car. But Greg got away from me, and I got mad." He looked at me. "So I hid from him. It was dark in the alley. I was going to jump out at him, scare him. I thought being alone in the dark would teach him a lesson.

"I heard a sound," James continued. "It was like a door slamming. Then I heard footsteps—someone else in the alley. I couldn't see him from where I was hiding. But I could hear him. And I could see Greg from where I was hiding. I heard footsteps coming closer—and I guess Greg thought it was me. Before I could do anything, I heard him yell, 'Freeze, you're dead!' That's when I heard a shot. Then another. Greg thought he was being smart. He thought he could scare me. But instead he startled the man . . . and the man shot him. I saw the gun. I saw Greg fall."

I looked him in the eyes. "Did you see the man at all, James? Did you get a look at his face?"

James looked at the floor. He shook his head.

The room was silent.

Then his dad said, "You said you saw what happened. You said you saw the man."

Eddy Leonard shook his head. "It wasn't me. I swear it wasn't me."

"You said you saw him," James said. "You told me what he looked like. You said he was the one. So I—"

"You gave the police the description your dad gave you," I said.

James's eyes were glistening. He looked at his father. "I said what you told me. I couldn't tell you what really happened. I thought you'd be mad. I tried to look after him, Dad. But you know how he could be. He ran away from me. I'm sorry. I'm so sor—"

Smack! Mr. Derrick slapped James hard, sending him reeling. Derrick was holding the gun and his cane in the same hand.

"James!" I said. "James, you can't do this. You can't let him do this. It's wrong. It's—"

James lunged at his dad and tried to wrench the gun from his hand.

Blam!

I jumped. James and his dad stood staring at each other, their faces white. James reached for the gun again and pulled it without resistance out of his father's hand. He gave it to me.

"Get it out of here," he said. Tears trickled down his face as he turned back to his dad.

"I'm sorry," he said.

Mr. Derrick leaned heavily against the counter, his head bowed. Eddy Leonard looked at me and at the gun in my hand. He staggered to his feet.

I carried the gun out of the house, went straight to James's car, and retrieved my phone from the backseat. It was turned off—and I'd promised my father that I would keep it on. I switched it on. There were three messages, all from my dad. I dialed his number. My hands were shaking.

"Robbie," he said when he answered. "I've been trying to reach you. Are you okay?" I barely noticed the urgency in his voice. I was just glad to be speaking to him.

"I have a gun," I said. "It's loaded. I don't know what to do with it."

"A gun? What's going on? What happened?"

"I'm outside," I said. "At James's place near Harris. James and his dad are inside. Dad, Eddy Leonard is here."

"Are you hurt, Robbie?"

"No."

"Is anyone hurt?"

"No, I don't think so."

"The police are on their way. They should be there soon."

It didn't occur to me to ask how that could be.

"Don't hang up. Stay on the phone with me until the police arrive," he said. "We'll be there in twenty minutes."

It didn't occur to me to ask who he meant by "we," either.

"Are you safe, Robbie? Is anyone threatening you?"

"No, Dad."

"Is there a place you can put the gun until the police get there? Somewhere no one will be able to find it?"

There was an outcropping of rocks a few feet away. I walked over to it and hid the gun between two enormous boulders.

Eddy Leonard came out of the house and blinked in the late morning sun.

"Are you okay?" he called to me.

I nodded.

He hovered on the porch, uncertain, until he came down the steps and stood on the dust and gravel.

"The police are coming," I said.

"I didn't do anything."

"I know."

The house behind him was silent. Neither James nor his dad had emerged. I started across the yard toward the porch.

"You should stay clear," Leonard said. "That man, the father, he's carrying around a lot of hate."

I think that's why I climbed the porch steps. I had seen that hate. I had seen what it had driven him to do. They were in there, just the two of them, and it was too quiet.

I opened the door and went inside. James was sitting on the stairs in the front hall, his head in his hands, his elbows on his knees. He looked up when I came through the door, and I saw that he had been crying.

"Where's your dad, James?"

James stared blankly at me for a moment before he said, "In the kitchen, I think."

"Are you okay?" I said.

"I should have been watching him. If I'd been watching him, if I hadn't played that stupid trick on him, he would still be alive. It never would have happened."

"You don't know that, James."

"Yes, I do," he said. "I do." His face was ashen. His eyes looked huge. "I wasn't driving that day," he said.

"What are you talking about? What day?"

"My dad was driving. We'd just come back from the cemetery, from visiting my mom. He was so different, Robyn. After my mom died, he was so different. He hardly ever spoke to me. He hated me, I know he did. He said he didn't want to live anymore. He said he'd lost everyone important to him—that he had no reason to live. He was driving the car when it crashed—my dad, not me."

I stared at him. He couldn't possibly be telling me what I thought he was telling me.

"I was in the hospital for a long time. So was my dad," he said. "I think that's when he decided. He wanted to come back here. He wanted to get the guy who shot Greg. And he wanted me to help him. He said I owed him." He shook his head. "We moved back to town, and I came up here in the summer and followed Leonard around. I found out about his habits, what he did, so that my dad could figure out how to get him to our place."

He let out a long, mournful sigh. "When my dad got that job in Australia, I thought that was the end of it. I'd go with him, make sure he got settled. Then I'd go to college somewhere. I'd make a new life. I didn't know he was going to be here today, Robyn. I told him I was coming up here with you to clean the place, like he wanted. But he didn't tell me he was going to be here. You have to believe me. I didn't know what he was going to do."

"I believe you, James." I glanced down the hallway that led to the back of the house. Then I heard the sound of a car approaching and went to the door to look out. My phone was still in my hand. I lifted it to my ear.

"Dad? The police are here."

"That's good," my dad said. "We'll be there soon, Robbie, I promise."

. . .

The police, two of them in a cruiser, arrived before my dad did. I told them what had happened and showed them what I had done with the gun. They secured the weapon in their cruiser and then radioed someone before going into the house. A few minutes later they escorted James and his dad out into the sun. They handcuffed Mr. Derrick and eased him into the back of the cruiser. One of them took James aside to ask him some questions while the other one took a statement from Eddy Leonard. I sat on the porch steps, waiting for my turn.

I spotted my dad's car while the two officers were still taking statements from James and Eddy Leonard. My dad wasn't alone. Nick was with him. They pulled up alongside James's car. My dad got out first. The cop who was talking to Leonard marched over to my dad, who showed some him ID. When the cops looked at Nick, I heard my dad say, "He's the boyfriend." I glanced at Nick to see what he thought of that description. Our eyes met, and my heart raced. He didn't look angry. Instead, he looked worried—worried and relieved. My dad said something else I didn't catch, and the next thing I knew Nick was hurrying toward me. I thought he was going to hug me. I ached to hug him. But he stopped half a pace away from me and said, "Are you okay?"

I nodded.

"What are you doing here?" I said. His face clouded. "I mean, what made you and my dad come up here?"

"Mac called me after you left this morning," Nick said. "He'd read my letter. He asked me to come up and talk. He wanted to know why I was leaving, make sure that I had someplace to stay. He's a good guy."

My dad had finished talking to the cop and stood leaning against his car—waiting, I think, until Nick and I were done.

"He had all these papers spread out on the dining-room table—stuff from the newspaper."

He must have meant the file that my dad's friend had sent over.

"There was a picture with one of the articles," Nick said. "I recognized him." He nodded to where James was, on the porch with a cop. "I told your dad that I'd seen you with that guy, but that you'd said his name was

James. He got worried when he couldn't reach you. The cops up here told him where this place was. He wanted to make sure you were okay."

"And you came up with him," I said.

"Yeah, well, your dad's a calm guy. Nothing ever seems to bother him. When he got worried, it kind of scared me." He stepped closer to me. "Maybe we don't have all that much in common, Robyn. Maybe nothing. But—" He came even closer, so that I had to crane my neck to look up into his eyes. "The thing is, it scared me that something bad might happen to you. You mean a lot to me, Robyn. I—" He shook his head. "I don't want to fight anymore."

I had spent the past year waiting for Nick—waiting for him to tell me what he was thinking, waiting for him to come back to me, waiting for him to take the lead. But I couldn't wait any longer. Maybe I would turn out to be wrong. Maybe it was too late. But I had to take that chance. I slipped my arms around his waist. It felt right. He smiled and drew me closer. We just stood there for a moment, holding each other, and I didn't care that my dad was watching. Then Nick pulled back just enough that he could look at me.

"I couldn't believe it when I ran into Danny in the summer. She used to be my best friend, and—" He peered deep into my eyes. "When I saw her, I don't know, I thought . . . I don't know what I thought exactly. I was just glad that she was back in my life. I wanted to hang out with her. But when she kissed me . . . I told her

187

how much she means to me, Robyn. But I don't love her. I don't feel the same way about her as I do about you. Not even close."

My heart raced. I stared up into his eyes and knew he was telling me the truth.

"I want us to be together."

"Me too," I said.

#1 Last Chance

Robyn's scared of dogs—but she agrees to spend time at an animal shelter anyway. Robyn learns that many juvenile offenders also volunteer at the shelter—including Nick D'Angelo. Nick has a talent for troublemaking, but after his latest arrest, Robyn suspects that he might be innocent. And she sets out to prove it . . .

#2 You Can Run

Trisha Hanover has run away from home before. But this time, she hasn't come back. To make matters worse, Robyn blew up at Trisha the same morning she disappeared. Now Robyn feels responsible, and she decides to track Trisha down . . .

#3 Nothing to Lose

Robyn is excited to hang out with Nick after weeks apart. She's sure he has reformed—until she notices suspicious behavior during their trip to Chinatown. Turns out Nick's been doing favors for dangerous people. Robyn urges him to stop, but the situation might be out of her control—and Nick's . . .

#4 Out of the Cold

Robyn's friend Billy drags her into volunteering at a homeless shelter. When one of the shelter's regulars freezes to death on a harsh winter night, Robyn wonders if she could've prevented it. She sets out to find about more about the man's past, and discovers unexpected danger in the process . . .

#5 Shadow of Doubt

Robyn's new substitute teacher Ms. Denholm is cool, pretty, and possibly the target of a stalker. When Denholm receives a threatening package, Robyn wonders who's responsible. But Robyn has a mystery of her own to worry about: What's with the muddled phone message she receives from her missing ex-boyfriend Nick?

#6 Nowhere to Turn

Robyn has sworn that she's over Nick. But when she hears he needs help, she's too curious about why he went missing to say no. Nick has been arrested again, and the evidence doesn't lean in his favor. When Robyn investigates, she discovers a situation more complicated than the police had thought—and more deadly. . .

#7 Change of Heart

Robyn's best friend Billy has been a mess ever since her other best friend Morgan dumped him. To make matters worse, Morgan started dating hockey star Sean Sloane right afterward. Billy is an animal rights activist—he wouldn't hurt a fly. But when Sean winds up dead, can Robyn prove Billy's innocence?

#8 In Too Deep

Robyn should be having the time of her life. She has a great summer job and a room in Morgan's lake house. But suddenly Nick appears in town—on a mission. He promised a friend he'd investigate a local suicide. Did Alex Richmond drown himself? Or was he killed because he knew too much?

#9 At the Edge

Robyn just wants to spend time with Nick, but he's always busy. Morgan thinks James Derrick, a hot transfer student, could take Nick off her mind. But James has problems of his own. When Robyn realizes she and James share a hidden connection, she starts to dig deeper. But is she digging her own grave?

ABOUT THE AUTHOR

Norah McClintock is the author of several mystery series for teenagers and a five-time winner of the Crime Writers of Canada's Arthur Ellis Award for Best Juvenile Crime Novel. McClintock was born and raised in Montreal, Quebec. She lives in Toronto with her husband and children.